Tanya's
DESERT STAR

written by
Linda Armstrong

cover design by Michael Petty

Tanya's
DESERT STAR

*In memory of
my brother, Don Keck*

First printing by Willowisp Press 1997.

Published by PAGES Publishing Group
801 94th Avenue North, St. Petersburg, Florida 33702

Printed in the United States of America

Willowisp Press®

2 4 6 8 10 9 7 5 3 1

ISBN 0-87406-867-3

chapter
ONE

DEFINITELY a nightmare, Tanya Marin thought. She leaned her head on the van window and pretended to sleep. Her neck hurt, but it was better than trying to talk. She knew if she tried, she'd only end up complaining or crying. And she didn't want to do either of those things in front of someone who was practically a complete stranger. Even if Aunt Laura was her mother's best friend, Tanya didn't know her that well.

The tall saguaros and low scrub of the Arizona desert whipped by the window. Actually, the wind was doing most of the whipping. Huge, dusty gusts assaulted the window glass. Out of the corner of her eye she noticed the speedometer needle of Aunt Laura's van hovering over the sixty-five mark, but the landscape outside didn't seem to move. The same scorched, brown plain, dotted with dusty, green cacti, rolled out endlessly toward the same range of rocky, purple hills.

Before Tanya had left, she had looked up "Phoenix, Arizona" in the encyclopedia at home. She knew that when she started Westside Middle School in the fall, she would have to write about her summer and she wanted to get all the gruesome details right. One of the bad things about being eleven years old was that you were still young enough to have to write summer-vacation essays but you were definitely old enough to be bored with them.

According to the encyclopedia article, Phoenix was named after a magical bird that burned up, then rose from its ashes. Looking at this place, Tanya could believe the part about the ashes.

She closed her eyes. *This has to be a nightmare,* she repeated to herself. *Nothing this awful could be real.*

She pictured waking up in her pink bedroom back home, slipping on her tiger slippers, and padding down the stairs to breakfast. That was the way it had been every morning since last April when they moved into their new house in California, and that was the way her mother promised it would be every morning forever—or at least until Tanya went to college.

The van lurched and she opened her eyes. She had actually managed to fall asleep, but unfortunately the bedroom at home in California had only been a dream. Arizona was real. The endless plain had given way to a suburban string of fast-food shops and super-markets, but it was still desert.

Aunt Laura turned off the main highway and onto a narrow street. The road curved up onto a low hill. Near the top, Aunt Laura maneuvered the van into the driveway of a big, coral-colored house.

"Tah dah!" she announced. "Here we are. Casa Linda Vista, the House of the Beautiful View."

Tanya's last hope evaporated like the mist from the neighbor's sprinkler, which hit the windshield and then disappeared. It was real all right—the whole ugly mess. Her mom had taken off for Taiwan to make *the* movie of her career and had left Tanya stuck in the middle of the Great American Desert for the summer.

As bad as it was, Tanya might have been more willing to give this Phoenix thing a chance if it hadn't been for the puppy.

Tanya had wanted a dog for as long as she could remember, but she and her mom moved too much. Her father had been killed in a car accident when she was four, and her mother had been supporting them with her acting career. Sometimes they had plenty of money and could afford a nice place. Other times they were broke.

First, they had lived with Grandma in her apartment in Santa Barbara. Then Grandma married a violinist and sold her house to travel with him. Tanya's mom got a small part in a soap opera, so they moved to a rented house in West Hollywood.

After that came an apartment with a swimming pool, then one on the fifth floor of a smelly building with no elevator, then one with two bedrooms and a fireplace. None of the places allowed pets.

Tanya remembered how her mom promised she would get a puppy when things settled down and they could buy a house. She also remembered what happened when they finally did.

Her mom called her in and gave her a hug. "We just can't have a puppy with white rugs. You understand that, don't you, honey?"

She had been nine then, and she did understand. She was never going to have a dog. Even when they moved to Sierra Madre, to a house with a tweedy, green carpet in the living room and a fenced-in yard, she didn't ask for a puppy. It would have been too hard if her mom said "no."

That's why it was such a surprise—almost a miracle— when Jackie, their new neighbor, came over with exciting news. Her German shepherd had had a litter and she was giving away the pups. They were two months old and, according to Jackie, would grow up to be big dogs that would enjoy living outside.

Tanya couldn't believe it when her mom said that they could have one. She said it would be a good watchdog. She even said that Tanya could pick the one she wanted right away.

Tanya couldn't even feel her feet on the ground as she followed Jackie back to her house to claim her little puppy. There in a box by the water heater were four bundles of brown fur. When one of them yawned a sleepy yawn and stood up lazily, Tanya knew immediately that was the one for her.

Tanya's mom was on the phone when she came back with the puppy, gently cradled in the crook of her arm. Mrs. Marin held up her hand in a gesture Tanya knew meant she would have to wait a minute.

"Yes, yes, of course," her mother was saying. "That

will be fine. My daughter will be out of school by then and I have a friend in Arizona who would be happy to help. Certainly. See you then." She set the phone carefully back in its cradle, then jumped up in the air like a kid and yelled, "YIPPEEE! I got it! The best script in years—Academy Award potential—and I got the lead!" Then her mom's gaze fell on the puppy wiggling in Tanya's arms.

"It's a girl, and I'm going to name her Lucky," Tanya said.

Suddenly, Tanya's mother looked sad. "Honey," she said. "I know I told you—"

Tanya shook her head. She knew what was coming next. "Oh, Mom! Please! Not again!"

"You'd better take her back before you two get too attached to each other."

"But, Mom, you promised," Tanya protested.

"I didn't know about the part then, honey, or that I'd have to be gone the entire summer. It's just not a good time right now. There will be other puppies."

"Sure, Mom," Tanya said softly. There was no use in arguing. She couldn't win, no matter how right she was. She took the puppy back and set it gently in the box.

Jackie asked what was wrong, but Tanya's throat was too tight to talk, so she just shook her head and ran back home, all the way to her room.

She slammed the door behind her, sprawled across the bed, and cried until she had no more tears left. Then she got out her dog books and leafed through them, imagining what it would be like to have a cocker spaniel curled up beside her, or a big black Lab, or a poodle—anything not to remember Lucky's soft, warm, little body in her arms.

She promised herself that when she grew up, she'd have a big ranch and twenty dogs.

"Tanya? Are you okay?"

Aunt Laura's question broke her out of her daze.

She sat up straight, pressed her palms into her cheeks, and wondered how long she had been sitting there drifting. "Oh, sure, just a little tired, I guess. I didn't get much sleep last night," she said.

Her answer, though not the whole truth, seemed to satisfy Aunt Laura, who nodded sympathetically. "I always have trouble sleeping the night before a trip. We're home now, anyway. You can take a nap if you want to."

"Maybe I will," said Tanya. She opened the van door and a wave of 112-degree air smacked her in the face. She gasped.

Aunt Laura laughed. "Really something, huh? The only ones who take to it right away are the reptiles." She opened the back of the van and pulled out Tanya's bags.

Aunt Laura picked up the big suitcase and started up the steep path to the house. Juggling her smaller rolling case and shoulder slung carry-on, Tanya followed. The pavement was so hot, it burned her feet through the soles of her shoes. With every step she became more convinced she was not going to be able to make it through this summer.

Tanya dropped her bags halfway up the path and sat down on the carry-on. She stared down at the silver van and the neatly arranged new housing development that covered Jackrabbit Hill. Curving streets led to dozens of other houses much like her aunt's. Several had gleaming, blue swimming pools. A few had transplanted trees. But it all looked a little artificial. Nothing looked as if it belonged in this wasteland.

In an instant Aunt Laura was at her side, encircling her with a strong, sure arm. Tanya could smell her spicy suntan lotion. "What's wrong, honey?" she asked.

"Nothing, Aunt Laura," Tanya said.

"Just call me 'Laura,' please. We both know I'm not really your aunt. It's enough for me to be your friend, don't you think?"

Tanya shrugged. She hated questions that weren't really questions. "Okay, Laura. It's okay, really. I guess I'm just hot."

"When we get inside you can help me make lemonade. How does that sound?"

It sounded terrible, but Tanya nodded and picked up the suitcases.

How could she explain that she felt all alone in the whole spinning universe? Laura meant well, but she was a stranger. The house was nice enough, but it wasn't home.

The real problem was worse. Tanya wasn't sure there *was* such a thing as home.

chapter

TWO

"**TANYA!**" called Aunt Laura from downstairs. Tanya stretched herself out on the small bed in the room that was hers for the summer and tried to ignore the call. The nap had helped, but it hadn't helped enough. She was still here, after all. Maybe if she closed her eyes again, it would all go away.

"Tanya," Aunt Laura's voice rang out again. "Come on down."

"I'll be there in a second, Aunt Laura—I mean, Laura," she called, but she didn't move an inch. It was hard for Tanya to stop thinking of Laura without the "aunt" part first. She was a friend all right, but she was her mother's friend, not Tanya's.

Laura and Tanya's mom had been in the same sorority in college. Tanya overheard them talking on the phone about a time when her mother saved Laura's life. When Tanya asked about it, her mom only laughed and said it was ancient history. It had sounded a lot more interesting than ancient history, and Tanya decided to ask Laura about it when she knew her better.

"Tanya! There's someone down here who'd like to meet you," Laura called again. No use delaying any longer. Tanya sat up in bed. The late afternoon sun streamed through the narrow blinds. The room glowed like some weird rain forest, the whole thing done in shades of green. Even the chest of drawers had been painted antique olive. Houseplants sat on every table, and some hung in the window. The room was a cool contrast to the dusty desert outside.

She yawned and glanced at the clock. It was almost four. "Just a minute," she called, slipping into her shoes. She tucked in her T-shirt and checked herself in the mirror. She scooped up her long, brown hair with the back of her hands and brought her elbows up toward her ears, imitating one of her mother's famous poses. Then she pulled her hair back in a ponytail.

People said someday she'd be as beautiful as her mother. She hoped not. People stared and gawked at her mother all the time. That wasn't Tanya's idea of fun.

Laura was in the living room. A girl about Tanya's age sat on the couch and sipped lemonade from a tall glass. She wore fringed denim cutoffs and a tank top. Her blond hair and tan complexion made her eyes the deepest blue Tanya had ever seen.

"Oh, there you are!" said Laura. "This is Autumn. She's a friend of mine."

"Hiya!" the girl said, standing up. "Laura's told me all about you! You have got to tell me all about Hollywood. It's got to be exciting, especially compared to this

14

place. Have you met any movie stars?" the girl asked, her words coming nonstop.

Tanya nodded. "I've met a few. They're mostly just regular people."

Autumn looked disappointed.

Tanya shrugged. "Where do you live?"

"At the end of the cul-de-sac just before this one. Want to come over and goof off?"

Tanya looked over at Laura, who nodded and made a slow, turning gesture with her hands to urge Tanya on.

"Sure, why not?" Tanya said.

Tanya followed Autumn out the door. The air smelled like the inside of a clothes dryer and the heat almost felt good after being in the air-conditioned house. They started down the path. "What grade are you in?" Tanya asked.

"Sixth next year. First one at the middle school here," Autumn answered.

"Same here," said Tanya.

"I know. Laura told me. That's why I was anxious for you to get here," Autumn said, walking a little faster so she was ahead and Tanya couldn't see her face. "Do you mind if I ask you something?"

"What?" Tanya asked, puzzled.

Autumn stopped and turned around. "Are you afraid of middle school?"

Tanya stared. "Are you kidding?" she asked.

Autumn shook her head. "I wish. I didn't want to admit it to anybody—but I've got to know. Am I the

15

only girl in the world who's afraid of getting hopelessly lost in the maze of middle school?"

Tanya picked up a white stone from a nearby gravel driveway and tossed it down the sidewalk. It had been a long time since she'd had a conversation like this with a friend. In fact, it had been a long time since she'd had a real friend. Here was a girl she just met who was saying something she had been feeling for months. In a strange way, Tanya felt relieved, as if she had been locked up and someone just opened the door.

"You're not the only one. I've changed schools every year. You'd think I'd be used to it, but I'm not. I'm still scared. This time it's worse because I'm going to have different teachers for all of my classes."

"I'm going to have five," said Autumn, "but one's gym."

"I hate gym," said Tanya.

"I don't. I'm going to run track. Maybe I'll even be in the Olympics someday. I have some friends helping me. They're called the Roadrunners. I hope you'll have a chance to meet them while you're here."

"Are they a track club?" Tanya asked.

Autumn laughed. "Not exactly," she said.

Tanya didn't have time to ask anything else about the Roadrunners because they had reached Autumn's house. It was almost like Laura's, but it was tan instead of coral, and it had a garage with an apartment over it. The apartment had studio windows on the desert side.

"This is going to sound dopey, but we have to be

16

quiet until five. That's when my dad stops working," Autumn said. She pointed to the apartment. "He plays music up there loud enough to wake the dead, but if I even bounce a ball out here between nine and five, watch out." She drew her finger across her neck.

"I know what you mean. My mom's that way when she's rehearsing. What does your dad do?"

"He's a painter. He does big foamy-looking pictures for a gallery in Scottsdale. I think they're weird, but what do I know? People buy them. Anyway, come on in here. I have something to show you." She opened the door to a cool, musky-smelling storeroom.

Tanya heard a sharp bark, followed by a chorus of tiny whimpers. There, in the corner of the room, standing beside a wicker basket, was the most amazing, elegant-looking dog she had ever seen. It had golden hair, a long, pointed muzzle, and big dark eyes. It wagged its tail cautiously as the girls entered the room.

Then Tanya gasped as three half-asleep puppies stumbled around her feet. There was a golden one, a white one, and a black one with a white spot between its eyes.

"Oh, my gosh," Tanya said.

"Come meet them," said Autumn. "They don't bite." Autumn sat down on the worn rug that covered most of the cement floor and picked up the golden puppy and looked into its eyes. "You are a sweetie, aren't you?" she said, as the tiny dog bathed her with kisses.

The mother dog greeted Tanya with majestic

17

sweeps of her long, feathered tail. Tanya patted her silky fur. "She's gorgeous! What's her name?" she asked.

"Scherazade," Autumn replied, still snuggling the golden pup. "She is beautiful, isn't she?"

Tanya nodded. "Scherazade," she repeated. "Such a strange name. What made you think of it?"

"She's a Saluki. Her ancestors were royalty in ancient Arabia, weren't they, Baby?" Autumn turned as she spoke to the mother dog.

Scherazade barked twice, then made whining noises. If Tanya hadn't known better, she would have sworn that the dog was trying to talk.

"Scherazade, sure," Tanya said. "I remember an old movie about her. Wasn't she the Arabian princess who told stories for a thousand-and-one nights so the sultan wouldn't cut off her head?"

"That's the one," Autumn answered.

"I always liked that story because Scherazade wasn't just beautiful. She was smart. She used her brains to save her own life."

Autumn put the puppy down and fixed her blue eyes on Tanya. "You know, you're right. In most stories like that one, the princesses get to live happily ever after because they are beautiful, not because they are smart."

Tanya watched, entranced, as the golden puppy trotted back to the basket and started gnawing on the white one's ear.

"You know, it just isn't fair!" Autumn said suddenly.

18

"What isn't?" Tanya asked, totally confused.

"You coming here this summer, of all summers." She stood up and dusted herself off.

Tanya scrambled to her feet. "Did I say something wrong? I'm sorry."

"No, no. I'm the one who's sorry. I like you. That's the problem," Autumn said, as she refilled the big, ceramic dog water dish from the faucet at the laundry sink.

"I don't get it," said Tanya.

"My family is going to Europe this summer. My dad has this stupid grant and it's supposed to be the experience of our lives or something. Don't get me wrong—I'd love to go to Europe, but not when my dad has a grant. I know him. We did one of these things two years ago in Vermont. He works the whole time. Mom goes shopping and I'm stuck in the hotel watching old shows on TV. At least in Vermont, *Gilligan's Island* was in English."

"Oh," said Tanya. She didn't know what else to say.

"Before you came, it was pretty bad, but not terrible. There aren't many other girls up here on the hill, and summer isn't the best season in Arizona, as I'm sure you've noticed. But now you're here, and I can see how much fun we'd have—and I'm so mad I could jump up and down and scream." Autumn's tanned face flushed purple.

"I feel the same way. Maybe we should both jump up and down and scream."

Autumn thought about it for a minute. "We can't. It

would scare the dogs. They're very sensitive."

"I was just kidding," said Tanya.

"I wasn't," said Autumn. "I do things like that sometimes."

"Screaming and jumping up and down?" Tanya asked.

"Sometimes, when I'm by myself," Autumn replied.

"It must be hilarious," Tanya said

"It is. I almost always end up laughing." She paused. When she spoke again, her voice was so soft Tanya could hardly hear her. "It's so weird. You just came today, and I feel like we've been friends forever. I wish . . . I wish I didn't have to go to Europe."

Tanya just shook her head sadly. Within a few moments, she felt as if she had found a friend—a friend who would help keep her loneliness away. And then, just as suddenly, it was snatched away from her.

It always happened this way, just the way it had with Lucky and a million other things in her life.

"I wish you were going to be here, more than anything," Tanya said at last.

They stood for a moment and watched the dogs. Scherazade nuzzled Autumn's hand. The puppies growled and rolled around in their basket, nipping and pawing at each other.

"Wait a minute," said Autumn. "Maybe I don't have to go."

Tanya shook her head. "What do you mean? How can you get out of it?"

"I've got this yucky cousin—Jeff—who helps Dad

out in the studio. He was going to watch the dogs while we were gone. Anyway, he's been bugging me about going in my place. At first I thought he was just kidding, but the way he's been bugging me, I don't think so. He'll be thrilled, and my dad will be happy, too. And Jeff loves museums. The two of them would camp out there if it weren't for the guards," Autumn said, talking so fast she hardly took a breath.

"Where would you stay?" Tanya asked.

"I could stay at Laura's. She has three bedrooms, and she's always telling me I'm welcome anytime," Autumn said.

Tanya's heart beat faster. "Do you really think your parents will go for it?"

"They'll try to talk me out of it, but my mom remembers Vermont. She'll understand," Autumn said.

Tanya smiled at her new friend.

Maybe this summer wasn't going to be so bad after all.

chapter
THREE

"N.T.," Tanya called from the upstairs bathroom. "Do you have a beach towel I can borrow?"

"Sure, Pony, on the top shelf of the cupboard above the sink." Laura had started calling Tanya "Pony" the third day after she got there, because she wore her hair in a ponytail all the time. Tanya called Laura "N.T." It was sort of a take-off on "auntie." It was fun, and Tanya liked it most of the time. But now, with Autumn moving in, she wondered if it was too immature.

Tanya used a folding stepstool to reach the shelf. Sure enough, there were several beach towels. She passed up one that had cartoon characters on it and took one with red stripes. "Are you going to call me Pony when Autumn moves in?" she shouted from the hallway on the way back to her room.

There was a moment of silence. "I'm sorry, Tanya. I thought you liked it," Laura replied. "I was just trying to make you feel more at home."

Tanya walked halfway down the stairs. From there, she could see Laura's worktable in the dining room. It was the same worktable where Laura had designed the famous "Little Orphan Alligator" dolls. Tanya's mother had said that those stuffed alligators earned Laura enough stock in Melvin Toys to retire at the age of thirty-two. Now she worked mostly for fun or for charity. Laura swiveled her chair and looked up at Tanya. She looked sad.

Tanya felt terrible. "I do like it, N.T., or I would have told you if I didn't. I just don't know what Autumn'll think."

"She'll think it's normal. After all, I have a nickname for her too—Speedy," Laura said.

Tanya laughed. "Speedy? Really?"

"Sure," said Laura, "but if you want to go back to our real names, that's fine with me."

Tanya smiled. She was glad that Laura understood. She hurried to her room and put on a pair of sandals. She had said she would meet Autumn at ten. She was almost an hour late.

Autumn was stretched out on a lounge beside her pool. When Tanya arrived, she walked over and sat on the tiled edge, dangling her feet in the blue water. Tanya slipped off the denim shorts and T-shirt she wore over her bathing suit and sat down beside her. The water was cool, but it felt great.

"Guess what?" Autumn said.

"Uh, you wrote an essay about a Saluki and won a million dollars," said Tanya.

"No," Autumn said.

"You flew around Phoenix on a magic lounge chair

24

and you just landed," Tanya said.

"No," Autumn said, "but that's not bad. Much more imaginative."

"I give up," Tanya said.

"My parents are leaving for Europe early. Jeff and my dad want to take an extra day in New York and go to museums. That means I get to come to Laura's tomorrow," Autumn said.

"That's great," said Tanya, but even to her own ears, she didn't sound very enthusiastic. A dozen confused feelings buzzed inside her like bees. When she first heard the news that Autumn's parents were going to let her stay home from Europe, she was happy and excited. But then the whole thing started to sink in. She was used to being alone, and she kind of liked it. And when she wasn't alone, she had Laura. She liked having Laura all to herself.

Tanya jumped into the deep end of the pool. She plunged down and touched the bottom before she pulled herself toward the bright surface. She was alone under the water. It was a familiar feeling. Her head broke the surface and she shook the water out of her ears.

"Hey, what did you do that for?" Autumn asked.

"I was hot," Tanya yelled from the other end of the pool.

"Come back," Autumn said.

"Not yet," Tanya said. She dove back underwater and swam toward the shallow end, a dozen questions banging around in her head. What if she and Autumn didn't have as much in common as they seemed to?

What if they didn't get along?

When she finally climbed out of the pool, Autumn threw a towel at her. It was damp and it reeked of chlorine. Tanya picked it up and threw it back. It would have hit Autumn in the shoulder if she hadn't dived into the pool.

"Race you six laps," Autumn challenged. Tanya dived back in. All her doubts disappeared as she kicked and stroked herself through the resistant water.

Autumn won by an arm's length, climbed out, and collapsed breathless on the cement. Tanya followed, gasping and tingling all over. She wrapped herself in the striped towel and sat on the lounge.

When she finally caught her breath, Tanya said, "You weren't kidding about the Olympics. You're fast."

"You're not so bad yourself," said Autumn.

"We should do that every day," said Tanya.

Autumn nodded, but she seemed distracted.

"What's the matter?" Tanya asked.

"The man who owns the dog that fathered Scherazade's puppies is coming over to get his pick of the litter today."

"Why does he get to pick the one he wants first?"

Autumn shrugged. "That's just how it usually works. I know I should be more grown-up about this, but I just hate to give any of them up. They're so cute. I didn't know it would be so hard or I wouldn't have let Scherazade have the puppies in the first place."

Tanya adjusted the lounge back so she was lying down flat.

"Aren't you going to say something?" demanded Autumn.

Tanya opened one eye and looked at her, "Like what?"

"Like how could I even say that?" Autumn propped herself up on her elbows and glared at Tanya.

"Why?" Tanya closed her eye. "I almost had a puppy once. When I found out I couldn't have her, I didn't care at all about acting grown-up. I just wanted to throw things."

"Hmmm," said Autumn.

Tanya listened to Autumn pull over another lounge. It was good to have her close by. The warm desert air felt like a weightless blanket on her damp skin. She remembered Lucky and all the friends she had just started to make every time she and her mom moved away from their apartments. The memories hurt a little less. Maybe this time she would actually be able to make a friend for keeps.

* * * * *

Around lunchtime, the dreaded moment came.

The papa dog's owner looked like a Saluki himself. He was tall, thin, and elegant, even in his casual T-shirt and cut-off jeans. He wore thick glasses with old-fashioned gold frames. He had a neatly-trimmed moustache and a bald spot on top of his head.

Autumn led the way to the dog's cool lair. She talked the whole time, about how her father had sent her Scherazade when he taught for a semester in Saudi

27

Arabia. She explained how hard it had been to wait for the quarantine to end, almost as hard as waiting for her father to come back.

Tanya was fascinated. She hadn't heard the story before. She stored up some questions to ask Autumn later. This wasn't the time. She could tell her friend was talking a lot to keep herself from crying. She knew Autumn probably wasn't even aware of half the words coming out of her mouth.

Tanya had done plenty of nervous talking herself. The last time was at the airport when her mother had walked her to the departure gate. She had talked so fast there was no time between words for a sob to sneak in.

The tall man didn't really seem to be listening. He just nodded and smiled politely.

Autumn opened the side door and held it. The man gallantly motioned Tanya in first, then ducked into the dim room behind her. He walked right over to the puppy basket. Tanya glanced at Autumn anxiously, then crossed the fingers of both hands behind her back. *Don't let him take the gold one,* she thought. That one was Autumn's favorite.

Autumn leashed Scherazade and led her to the far corner of the little room. The mother dog seemed to know exactly what was going on. She strained at the short stretch of slender chain and whimpered. Autumn knelt down and stroked her delicate head.

"It's all right," she repeated again and again.

The man held up the puppies one at a time, feeling

their flanks, checking their eyes, and looking at their teeth.

"You've done a fine job here," he said. "This is the best litter I've seen yet. It's a hard choice, but I'll take the white one. I have a lady friend whose house is white inside and out. She'll love him."

Tanya uncrossed her fingers and sighed with relief. She glanced over at her friend. Autumn looked relieved, too.

The man shook Autumn's hand. They exchanged papers, then he scooped up the white pup and was gone.

"Now it's your turn," said Autumn softly after the door slammed behind him.

"What do you mean?" asked Tanya.

"One of the pups is yours," Autumn said motioning toward the basket where the two remaining puppies were curled up.

Tanya's heart beat wildly. She had trouble catching her breath.

"Don't kid around with me that way," she said

Autumn didn't look as if she was kidding. She knelt down and stroked Scherazade's head, but didn't unfasten the leash.

"When your mom called about having you spend the summer here, Laura thought you would be bored. Laura told your mom about the pups, so your mom sent money to reserve one."

"Was that okay with you?" asked Tanya.

Autumn nodded and smiled. "Your mother's check

paid for shots and food for all of them. There was even enough left to make my last payment to Scherazade's breeder."

Tanya remembered now. Her mother had promised her a surprise in Arizona.

Maybe things really are going to change, she thought. *Mom kept her promise.*

"Now I know why Aunt Laura left a dog magazine in my room with an article about Salukis," Tanya said as she walked over to the basket. She petted each of the pups. They licked her and gazed at her lovingly with their big, dark eyes. Finally she scooped them both up. She tucked the black one under her arm and held the golden one out to Autumn.

Her friend took the little dog and hugged it. "Are you sure that's the one you want?" she asked.

"Of course," Tanya said

"But . . . you don't have to leave me the best one," Autumn said. There were tears in her eyes.

"Actually, I didn't leave you the best one," said Tanya. "According to the article, the Arabs considered Salukis with spots on their foreheads to be the most special of all. The spot was called 'The Kiss of Allah.'"

"Wow," said Autumn, giggling at the golden puppy that was licking her ear.

"What are you going to name him?" Tanya asked after they unfastened Scherazade and settled the puppies down. Autumn pulled the storeroom door shut with a soft click and the two headed back in the sunlight back toward Laura's. Tanya couldn't wait to thank her for the hand she had in this.

"It's funny. I don't know. He has to have the perfect name—special, you know?"

Tanya nodded. "Like Scherazade," she said.

"What about you? Have you thought of a name yet?" Autumn asked.

Tanya thought about her puppy. In the days when she had only been wishing for a dog, she had collected pictures and made lists of names. Lucky had been a good name, but she couldn't use it. She would always think of Lucky as a little German shepherd, not a Saluki. None of the other names she had thought of seemed special enough.

"I asked you because I was hoping to get an idea," she said.

"I do have an idea," said Autumn mysteriously.

"About a name?" asked Tanya.

"No. About how to get one," said Autumn.

"How?" asked Tanya.

"From the wind," she replied.

Tanya shook her head. "The wind? That's weird. I think this heat is getting to you."

"I'm serious," Autumn said. "It's how I make my most important decisions."

"But there isn't any wind," Tanya protested. The air was so still it hummed.

"There's none now, but that will change." said Autumn, smug and smiling a little. "I'll come up after dinner and show you."

It sounded strange, but exciting. "Okay," Tanya said.

Laura was waving to them from the window. The path to the house was steep. Sweat poured down both sides of Tanya's face. A big, salty drop headed for the end of her nose.

They huffed and puffed all the way to Laura's porch. Laura met them at the front door. Tanya could tell from the look on her face that Laura knew Tanya had gotten the good news. Without giving a thought to the sweat dripping from her body, she gave Laura a huge bear hug.

chapter

FOUR

THE sun was setting, but the sky was still full of color when Autumn knocked on the door. "Ready?" she whispered.

"Ready as I'll ever be," said Tanya in her normal voice. Autumn put a finger to her lips. "If you talk like that, you won't be able to hear the words in the wind," she said.

"You really are nuts," said Tanya, but she followed her out beyond the paved cul-de-sac to a smooth rock overlooking the desert. Tanya started to say something, but Autumn put her finger to her lips and pointed to the rock. They sat down side by side.

The sky was dark blue with a line of red, the last trace of the day, outlining the western horizon. Tanya remembered all the times she had watched the sun set over the ocean, how it turned the water silver. As the sun set, the desert didn't shimmer like the ocean did. It glowed a rich gold.

The wind came as the last red faded. It gusted around them, rattling the brush. It picked up the strands of hair that had come lose from Tanya's ponytail and blew them across her eyes.

The wind whistled and whined like a sad, lonely animal, but Tanya could hear no words in it. She looked over at Autumn. Her friend was sitting very still, eyes closed, listening.

Tanya concentrated on the sky. High above their heads, the first star appeared. Venus had been visible long before the sun had set, but Venus didn't count. It was a planet, close and shining from reflected light. It didn't have the right kind of magic.

The first *real* star was different, twinkling under its own power across millions of miles of space.

The wind did have a voice then. It said one word as Tanya made her wish and gazed at the star. The word was "name," but she didn't know what it meant. A prickly bush nearby rustled. "Name, name, name," it whispered. Tanya kept her eye on the star, then began to understand. *Of course,* she thought. *Name.* That was what she had come here to find, a name for the pup.

The Arizona night was as black and soft as her puppy's fur. Other stars came out, a few at a time, until she could pick out some constellations. The shadowy Milky Way swept across them like a white scarf. After a while she couldn't remember which one had been the wishing star, but it didn't matter, because she already had what she came for.

The street light came on down the block, and Autumn stood up. They walked back to Laura's in silence. They didn't go into the house, but sat outside on the porch.

Autumn spoke first. "I got the name," she said. "It's the only name for Scherazade's son—Sheik of Dawn."

Tanya found it easy to imagine the golden puppy, full-grown, running in the half-light of morning, in charge of the world. It was the perfect name for him.

"I have a name, too," said Tanya. "I didn't think your trick would work, but it did. His name is Desert Star."

Autumn nodded. "That's it. Couldn't have been anything else. But it's better if you have three names when you register the puppy officially. How about, 'Tanya's Desert Star'?"

"Perfect," said Tanya. She thought for a minute, then added, "I think we should tell the puppies their names in a special place, don't you?"

"What a great idea!" said Autumn. "I know just the spot. I'll meet you out front here at six."

"Six?" Tanya repeated. "In the morning?"

"Sure. This place is best before it gets hot. I'll bring the dogs."

* * * * *

"Are we almost there?" asked Tanya. It was early morning and they were puffing around the curve to Hawk Point, a big rock outcropping at the edge of the Jackrabbit Hill development. Scherazade trotted obediently at Autumn's side. The two puppies ran out ahead on woven leads. They paused to taste every leaf

35

and sniff every bush.

"Almost," promised Autumn.

"You've been saying that for fifteen minutes," Tanya said.

"This time we really *are* almost there. The dogs know."

Scherazade started barking, and the puppies joined in with their sharp, little voices. The big rock formation at Hawk Point glowed pink in the early light. Something dark moved near the top of the rock.

Tanya shaded her eyes against the sun. A tall, skinny boy with bright red hair scampered above them on the rocks. He was wearing the typical shorts and T-shirt, but a large leather sack hung from his belt.

"Somebody's up there," Tanya whispered.

"That's not somebody. It's just Jacob," Autumn replied.

"I heard that," cried the redhead, and with a single bound from the rock, he landed in front of them, hands on his hips.

Tanya had never seen anybody with so many freckles. There was hardly any room between them for his skin.

"Catch anything today?" Autumn asked.

"Not much. A couple of lizards." He reached into the leather pouch and pulled out a limp, brown fence lizard.

"He's dead," said Tanya.

"Naw, that's his only defense. If I put him down, you'd see a miracle. He'd run so fast—" He paused and

36

looked directly at her. His eyes were bright green with little flecks of brown.

"Who are you?" he asked.

Tanya had to make an effort not to stare at those amazing eyes. Finally she managed to stammer out an introduction. "I'm Tanya, from L.A."

"I don't remember any moving vans this summer. I don't usually miss things like that," Jacob said.

"I haven't moved in. I'm just visiting," Tanya said.

"Visiting Phoenix in the summer? You must be nuts. The people around here head for the ocean or the mountains at the end of May and you don't see them again until September," Jacob said.

"*You're* here," Autumn observed, her arms folded across her chest.

"My family *is* nuts, and I can't drive yet. Besides, this is the best season for reptiles," Jacob said, stroking his captive with one finger.

Autumn turned to Tanya. "Jacob has this thing for snakes."

"Are there many snakes around here?" she asked softly, as if they might hear her and come out.

"Not as many as there used to be," Jacob said. "All these people, houses, and cars have scared them away. You have to go down to the desert, and even then you won't see too many out after the sun comes up. Snakes are shy. They don't like us any more than we like them."

Jacob held out his palm with the frightened lizard in it. Tanya touched its tiny head. It was cool and smooth. Jacob smiled at her. He had a great smile, wide and sincere, and it made deep dimples in his cheeks.

"Hey, want to come over and help me set up a new aquarium for these guys?" Jacob asked.

Tanya looked at Autumn. She wanted to see where Jacob lived, but she didn't want to seem too eager. Autumn didn't seem to notice Tanya's reaction. She rolled her eyes at Jacob. "Some other time," she said.

Jacob shrugged. "Suit yourself," he said. He put the lizard gently back into his bag and started toward the development along the path the girls had just taken. When he was out of sight, Autumn led Tanya and the dogs to a sheltered spot on the far side of the rock.

"Don't you like Jacob?" Tanya asked.

"He's okay," Autumn said.

"I think he's cute," Tanya said.

Autumn turned and stared at her. She was obviously trying not to laugh. "Cute? Jacob?"

Tanya felt her face get hot and she knew she was blushing.

Now Autumn really started laughing—and hard. "I don't believe it. You actually like Jacob Printer."

"I wouldn't want to go to the movies with him or anything. I just said I thought he was cute."

"Sure, sure," Autumn said knowingly, shaking her head. "You really should see his parents' place, though. It's a local landmark. Someday they're going to make it into a park and a nature museum. Jacob says he'll be the ranger, and he probably will."

38

"Well, maybe we should take him up on his invitation after all," Tanya said.

"We came up here to name the dogs, remember? I guarantee, we'll both see more of Jacob than we want to this summer. Besides, he did get a little goofy when you introduced yourself. Maybe he likes you, too."

"Do you really think so?" Tanya asked.

Autumn shook her head. "Movie Star meets Reptile Man. This is going to be a really weird summer."

"Cut it out and tell me about this place," said Tanya.

"Okay," said Autumn, suddenly serious. She sat down on a big rock and gathered the dogs around her. Tanya found a rock and sat down, too. Autumn was quiet for a minute. When she spoke, her voice echoed off the overhanging ridge. "This has been a special place for a long time. A friend of mine in the Roadrunners showed me how the first people who lived here ground corn on these rocks."

She pointed to several flat stones with depressions the size of small bowls worn into them. Tanya could imagine the strong, tanned women, talking and laughing as they worked. She could almost sense them hiding behind the bushes.

Autumn scooped up her golden pup and handed the black one to Tanya. "You go first," Autumn said.

Tanya could feel the pup's heart beating against her hand. She put him in her lap and he snuggled down.

Tanya stroked the puppy's silky fur. "Your name is Desert Star," she said, her own voice echoing around her. "You are the answer to a thousand wishes."

Autumn spoke next. She held her puppy up and looked into his eyes. "You are Sheik of Dawn. You are pure royalty, the most beautiful puppy in the world."

They sat for a minute, petting the dogs and listening to the early morning birds.

Suddenly the bushes behind them crackled. They both jumped to their feet, letting the confused pups jump to the sandy ground.

"What are you doing?" a young voice demanded. It was Jacob.

"Nothing that would interest you," said Autumn, turning to give Tanya a warning look.

"Girl stuff?" he asked.

"That's right," said Tanya. No matter how great his eyes were, Jacob had already spoiled the mood.

"Are you ready to come over and help me with the aquarium yet?" he asked.

Tanya shot Autumn her best pleading look.

"The dogs could play, too. Deborah loves company," Jacob nodded toward the pups.

"Deborah?" Tanya echoed.

Autumn rolled her eyes. "I'm afraid he has a Saluki, too."

"Well, what are we waiting for?" asked Tanya. "Let's go!"

Autumn put her head back as if asking the heavens for advice. "I give up," she said at last. "Yes, we're ready. Lead, oh Great One, we will follow."

"Great. Come on!" Without waiting a second, Jacob headed down the rise below the outcropping and bounded up a small hill on the other side.

The two followed Jacob with Sheik and Star in their arms. The dogs were exhausted from their early morning hike and had refused to walk or move on their own. The girls had no choice but to carry them.

"Come on, slowpokes," Jacob shouted to them from the top of the hill.

Tanya shifted her pup's weight to one side. His paws draped over her arm. She stroked his silky black head. He bathed her fingers with wet kisses.

"Go ahead," called Autumn. "We'll meet at your house."

"I'll just wait here," Jacob yelled. "I want to see Tanya's face."

"Why does he want to see my face?" Tanya asked.

"His house is a little . . . unusual. He loves to show it to people—especially to you, I think."

Tanya was fascinated, but she didn't want to seem too interested. "How much farther is it?" she asked.

"Just on the other side of the hill," Autumn said.

Tanya led the way to the shadier side of the street and walked a little faster.

Scherazade barked and danced in the driveway of one of the houses. A pale Saluki face appeared between the drapes in the front window.

"That's Terez," Autumn explained. "She belongs to Dr. Storik. You'll meet both of them on Saturday when we go out with the Roadrunners."

"You keep talking about the Roadrunners. Who are they?" Tanya asked.

"It's a club for Saluki owners here in Phoenix. Dr. Storik started it. I joined when my dad brought me Scherazade," Autumn said.

"I've never heard of a club for owners of a certain kind of dog," said Tanya.

"I think some other breeds of dogs have owners' clubs. They couldn't be as good as the Roadrunners, though," said Autumn.

"What's so special about these Roadrunners?" asked Tanya.

"First, we do really cool stuff. Not just dog stuff, but things that really help the community. Last year a developer was going to tear down a building that had been a historic stage-coach stop, and the Roadrunners held a big barbecue to help raise money to save it. This year we're working on a stuffed animal project for sick kids and their moms. That's how I got to know Laura. She's in charge of the stuffed animal project."

"Is Laura a Roadrunner?" Tanya asked.

"No, you have to have a Saluki, and she doesn't. We may make her our first honorary member, though."

"What else do you do?" asked Tanya.

"Well, it's mainly a club for the dogs. That's how it got started, and it's still the most fun. The dogs like to get together and run and play. They have as much fun together as we do."

Tanya was confused. Every club she had ever heard of met in a room. She didn't understand how dogs could run around together at a meeting. Wouldn't they knock over the furniture? "I don't get it," she said.

"Where do they run?"

"At the ranch," said Autumn, mysteriously.

"What ranch?" asked Tanya.

"Come on," yelled Jacob.

"You'll find out on Saturday," Autumn said, starting up the hill.

"What's happening Saturday?" Tanya asked, struggling to keep up.

"An initiation for a brand-new Roadrunner," Autumn said.

"An initiation?" Tanya asked. She had a feeling about who the new member was going to be, and she wasn't sure she felt entirely good about it.

"You know, a ceremony to make someone a member of the club," Autumn said.

"Like the dog-naming ceremony we just had?" Tanya asked, hoping it would be quick and simple.

"Not exactly," said Autumn. She whistled to Scherazade, who hesitated, sniffing the bulging green trunk of a palo verde tree and then dashed up to join them.

Jacob had been leaning against the rocky wall of the road cut at the top of the hill. He stood up, brushed himself off, and pointed down toward a rambling two-story farm house beside remnants of a dried stream bed. "There it is," he said.

Tanya could see what Autumn had meant when she said Jacob's place was unusual. The house was a ranch style, but an old-fashioned ranch style, like you'd see in an old western. The front yard was filled with rusty old farm machines and, from the top of the hill looking down, Tanya could see that the big red barn needed a new roof.

There weren't any fields around the house. Outside the weathered wooden fences that surrounded the place stretched miles and miles of Phoenix suburb— housing developments, apartments, and mini-malls.

"Come on, that's not your house. It's some kind of museum," said Tanya.

"Wanna bet?" Jacob asked, twitching his eyebrows up and down.

Tanya glanced at Autumn, who shook her head. "Don't bet him. He'll win. It really is his house."

Jacob rolled his eyes. "Okay, now that you've ruined my chances of winning a fortune, I'll give you the tour."

He led them down a trail between several yards, talking all the way. "We used to live in L.A., like you. Then my grandma died and left this place to us. Dad was sick of the city, so he said, 'Why not?' and we came without even seeing it. Turns out, Dad thought it would still be like it was when he visited it as a little boy. In those days the whole development on the other side of the hill belonged to my grandpa, only it wasn't a development then. It was a sheep ranch. On this side of the hill, just on the other side of the barn, were fruit and nut trees. My grandma made pies and sold them to tourists who drove out here from town on weekends for picnics."

"Was your dad surprised when he saw the way it is now?"

"Sure. Oh, he knew the land had been sold, but he

44

couldn't believe how the city had closed in on it. Mom wanted to go back to L.A., and so did my big sister, but Dad and I worked on them. You'll see. It may not be the country any more, but it's still a great place. The State of Arizona declared it a historical monument. We have a plaque and everything. We've been in the newspaper lots of times. Once we were even on TV."

Jacob unlatched the barn door and swung it open. A white Saluki with golden spots came bounding over to meet them.

"Say hi to Tanya, Deborah. She's from Hollywood," he said as he stroked his dog's sleek head.

Deborah barked and took off across the yard with Scherazade, Star, and Sheik close behind.

"Don't worry about them. They'll have a great time," Jacob said. He led the girls to the old barn and swung the door open. Light angled down in shafts through the high windows. The hard earth floor had been swept smooth and clean. Old furniture and stacks of dusty cardboard storage cartons filled the space under the loft at the far end. A four-wheel-drive van sat in the middle.

A long workbench occupied most of the front wall. Beside it sat rows of metal shelves. Some were filled with wire cages, others with glass jars and aquariums. Jacob dropped his pack on the bench.

"Now for the aquarium!" Jacob said, his eyes gleaming. Then he smiled his wide, dimpled smile and handed Tanya an empty coffee can. As he did, his hand lightly brushed hers. "Want to find me some dirt?"

Tanya felt her cheeks burning. She took the coffee can quickly, trying not to notice his eyes following her.

"Sure," she said, her voice quavering just a little. What was it about this weird freckle-faced kid and his room full of lizards that made her heart pound?

chapter
FIVE

IT had already been a long day. After all the activities with the dogs and getting the grand tour at Jacob's, the girls still had to come back and help Autumn's parents load their bags into the airport van.

When Autumn's parents rode away, it was still light outside. Tanya, Autumn, and Laura sat down to have their first dinner together. They watched television as they ate their spaghetti. Nobody said much. Tanya was hungry, hungrier than she had been in months. Autumn seemed far away. Tanya couldn't tell if she was sad about her parents leaving or if she was just totally involved in the quiz show they were watching.

Later, Tanya and Autumn sat together on the bed in Laura's guest room among the heaps of Autumn's clothing on the beige quilt.

"Do you know anything about those paintings on the wall?" Autumn asked Tanya, pointing to a group of paintings in shades of tan. They showed skinny, tall people with their heads facing to one side and their feet turned toward the center.

"Laura says they're copies of sand paintings," said Tanya. "She bought them on one of the Hopi mesas near Flagstaff."

Autumn nodded. "I've seen them before in some of the tourist shops in Scottsdale. I'm surprised Laura picked them. People around here are sick of Southwest art. Most of it is so fake."

"Not these. Laura said a Hopi healer told her these designs put people back in touch with themselves."

"Sure, the real ones might. We studied about it at school. The sand paintings are part of a ceremony. But it isn't the picture that supposedly does the healing. It's tradition and faith."

Tanya stared at Autumn. "A ceremony. Something like listening to the night wind for answers to your problems?"

"Sure, that's a ceremony, but it's not really a tradition," Autumn said, lying back on the bed, arms behind her head.

"Well, it's your tradition and I like it. I'm going to make it my tradition, too," Tanya said, as she pushed a hanger through one of the sleeves of Autumn's shirts.

Autumn smiled and sat up, leaning on one elbow. "I'm glad. I'm always afraid to share things like that with people."

Tanya leaned into the closet and hung up the shirt. Then she spoke softly, her back still to Autumn. "People? I'm not just people, am I?"

Autumn's answer was just what she'd hoped it would be. "I wouldn't be here now if you were," she said. "I'd be on that plane with my parents, headed for Europe."

Tanya turned around to see Autumn, cross-legged on the bed, folding shorts. "Are you going to miss them?" Tanya asked.

Autumn bit her lip and nodded. "I didn't think I was going to, but I already do."

"I know what you mean. I miss my mom, too. I'm mad at her, but I miss her."

Tanya sat down beside Autumn. They were quiet for a long time. Laura's sewing machine hummed downstairs and a plane flew over the house. Autumn hugged Tanya. Tanya sat very still. Finally, she gave her a quick hug back.

Autumn pulled away from the embrace and rushed into the bathroom that divided Tanya's room from hers. When she came back, Tanya noticed her eyes were red and puffy. Autumn picked up the clothes she had been folding and put them in a drawer.

"You've really thought about sand paintings and traditions a lot, haven't you?" Tanya asked, changing the subject from missing their parents back to the paintings.

Autumn hesitated. She seemed surprised by the question. "Well, sure. I told you, my dad's a painter, and I like to paint, too."

"I didn't know that," Tanya said.

Autumn did a neat somersault onto the bed, then she turned and faced Tanya. "This is going to sound weird, but . . . remember what you said about the princess Scherazade being smart instead of just pretty? That made me wonder if you have trouble being like your mom."

Tanya tried to avoid her friend's eyes. "What do you mean?" she asked softly.

"Your mom is beautiful. I saw her in a movie once. You look a little like her."

Tanya felt her face burning and knew she must be as red as the rocks at the edge of town. "So?" she asked.

"So, you have trouble looking like your mother. I have trouble loving art like my dad. Maybe it's not the same, but when he's around, I can hardly admit to anyone how much I like to draw and paint. It's almost as if he's going to yell at me about not being good enough, and that would hurt so much I don't think I could stand it. It's easier to think about other things."

"Like Salukis?"

Autumn nodded and smiled. "Like Salukis."

Tanya walked over to the window. She pulled aside the drapes. It was eight o'clock and the orange-red sun sat on the horizon like an over-cooked egg yolk. She pointed out toward the desert. "Is the ranch where the Roadrunners meet out that way?" she asked.

"Why do you do that?" asked Autumn.

"Do what?" asked Tanya, turning to face her, confused.

"Every time we talk about feelings, you change the subject. Why do you do that?" Autumn asked again.

Tanya turned back to the window. She wanted to

explain, but the words wouldn't come. She wanted to say how she felt every time she had to leave new friends—and how nobody ever wanted to hear about it.

Tanya thought about the friend she had made when she was five years old, just a year after her father had died. The little girl lived down the street from her grandmother's and the two loved to ride stick horses together. Tanya's horse was named Midnight because he was black. Tanya could remember the name of the girl's horse—it was Blue—but she couldn't remember the girl's name.

One afternoon, Tanya came home and found out they had to move. She immediately burst into angry tears and said every mean word she could think of. Her mother got mad at her. Then her grandmother got mad at her. They said she was being selfish. They sent her to her room and she had to sit there alone until all the tears and all the words were gone.

How could she explain to Autumn that the words were still gone?

Tanya watched the last edge of the sun disappear. The clouds glowed red, then yellow. She could feel Autumn watching the sunset over her shoulder. "You don't think you made the wrong choice, do you?" Tanya asked in a soft voice.

"About what?" asked Autumn.

"About staying," asked Tanya.

"Naw," said Autumn. "I told you. I wouldn't like *Gilligan's Island* in French." She grabbed a stack of books and handed them to Tanya. They worked in silence for a few minutes.

Strains of brassy jazz floated faintly up from downstairs, mixing with the hum of the sewing machine. Laura had told the girls she would be up late finishing a batch of stuffed animals for the Roadrunner project.

"Those pictures may not be the real thing, but they sure worked for me," Autumn said. "I'm not sure what getting in touch with yourself really means, but for me, it has something to do with painting."

Tanya hung three white blouses in the closet. "I don't think looking like my mom has anything to do with being myself," she said. Then she turned to face Autumn, who was arranging clothes in one of the drawers. "I am sorry I have trouble talking about people leaving. I guess I think it bothers other people as much as it bothers me. Anyway, I'm glad you're staying."

"I almost did change my mind, you know," Autumn said, sliding the last drawer shut and smoothing the comforter. "It's not you or Laura. I've just never been away from my parents for so long, and I'm a little scared."

Tanya nodded. "I knew that. That's the way I felt when I left my mom." Tanya paused for a second. "Let's go throw a ball for the dogs."

"In the dark?" asked Autumn.

"Sure," said Tanya. "There's a light in the driveway, isn't there?"

"Sometimes I think you're crazier about those dogs than I am. I bet you'd sleep outside with them if you could."

"Hey, do you think we could?" Tanya asked.

"Could what?" Autumn asked.

"Sleep outside with the dogs." Tanya said.

"You're hopeless," Autumn said. "Let's just throw them a couple of balls. Then we really should help Laura with the stuffed animals."

"Why don't we just take our real dogs to visit these sick kids instead of making all stuffed animals?" Tanya asked.

"Tanya, you're full of crazy ideas," said Autumn, as she grabbed a bag of used tennis balls from the hall cupboard and started down the stairs.

chapter
SIX

IT was eleven o'clock on Saturday morning, the day of the meeting of the Roadrunners. Autumn and Tanya sat on the curb waving folded paper fans at each other as they waited for Mrs. Hernandez to pick them up. Scherazade and the two pups snoozed in the shrinking shadow of Tanya's knees.

"I wonder if Miss Hernandez will be this late to class," Autumn said.

"To class?" Tanya asked.

"Yeah, she's going to be my history teacher next year," Autumn said.

"I thought you said you were afraid of middle school," said Tanya. "How can you be afraid when one of your teachers is a friend?"

"You don't know Miss Hernandez. She's tough," said Autumn.

"This is some club. A doctor, a teacher. Is everybody an important adult except us?" Tanya asked.

"Don't worry. There are other kids," said Autumn.

"What about this initiation?" Tanya asked.

"I can't tell you or it wouldn't be official," Autumn said. "You'll find out soon enough."

Tanya ran her hands over her jean-clad knees and stomped the street with the heavy hiking boots Autumn had insisted she wear. She had said it might be dangerous without them. That word—*dangerous*—kept echoing through Tanya's mind. She never did anything dangerous unless she had to. Ordinary living was dangerous enough without taking extra chances just for the fun of it. Besides, if it was dangerous for her, wouldn't it be dangerous for Star? He was still a puppy.

Once, in second grade, Tanya remembered, she had almost joined the Brownies. She went to one of their meetings, but she felt so weird there, she never returned. All the girls knew each other's names and had been to each other's houses. They knew the words to songs she had never heard before, and they knew how to do crafts she had never seen.

She knew from her experience with the Brownies that clubs had rules. If the Roadrunners were going somewhere dangerous, she knew they had to have lots of rules. What if she couldn't remember them all? What if she did something wrong and Star got hurt— or Autumn?

"I was just thinking," Tanya said. "Maybe you should go without me."

Autumn shook her head. "No way," she said. "It wouldn't be fair to Star. Besides, you'll love it. I promise."

"What if they don't like me?" Tanya asked.

Autumn rolled her eyes. "Give me a break."

"You don't understand, Autumn. Sometimes I get on people's nerves."

"No!" Autumn protested, like a bad actress hearing a shocking line.

"I mean it. I can't seem to keep friends," Tanya said. "One girl even told me I was a spoiled, stuck-up show-off. Maybe she was right."

"Well, you can be a little hard to live with, especially when you're pulling this excuse-me-for-living bit. But, believe me, the Roadrunners will be glad to have you."

Just then a gold-colored van swung around the curve into view. The faces of two Salukis peered out of both of the tinted side windows. Scherazade broke into a chorus of happy barks and danced out to the end of her leash.

The van pulled up in front of the girls, and a tall woman with wavy, black hair and cocoa-with-cream skin hopped out to open the sliding panel door.

"Thought you'd forgotten us today, Miss Hernandez," said Autumn.

"Sorry," said the tall woman. "I was just running a little late."

Tanya scooped up Star and stood. Her knees shook for a second. She couldn't tell whether it was from nerves or from sitting too long.

In the front passenger seat was a young woman with a long, dark braid. Her smile was a flash of light.

"This is Elaine Littlefeather and her Saluki, Marga," said Miss Hernandez. "She's working at the Intertribal

Council this summer. She heard about our club and wanted to join in the fun. I hope it's all right."

Tanya thought it was very strange for Miss Hernandez to be asking Autumn if it was all right to bring someone along.

Autumn didn't seem surprised at all. "Great," she said. "I've brought someone, too. This is my new friend, Tanya, from California. She's staying at Laura Michaels' house for the summer."

Tanya felt her face burn as the two smiling, adult faces turned toward her.

"Glad to meet you," Miss Hernandez said.

"We'd better get started or Dr. Storik, Bradley, and Jacob will get lost," said Autumn.

At the sound of Jacob's name, Tanya felt a little dizzy. There had been so much going on that she hadn't really thought about him lately. Now just the mention of his name brought back the image of his deep, dimpled smile and bright, piercing eyes.

She whispered to Autumn, "Is Jacob in the Road-runners, too?"

"Of course," Autumn whispered back.

The engine roared, and they were off down a dirt road Tanya hadn't noticed before. It went straight down into the desert. They didn't talk much after that because the road was rough and everything on the car rattled and banged. Also, every time one of the dogs spotted a rabbit, pack rat, or prairie dog along the way, they all barked joyously. The sound of five Salukis barking full-out was deafening. Autumn and Tanya, closest to the racket, put their hands over their ears and laughed.

Miss Hernandez's piece of land looked like all the rest of the desert for miles around. Tanya wondered how she could tell where it started and where it ended.

The van pulled over in a cloud of red dust. "Here we are. Welcome to Forty Acres," she announced. Elaine opened the door for the girls while Miss Hernandez unloaded the picnic chest and one of the water jugs.

The dogs didn't wait. All five romped off in a jumble of white, gold, and black.

Tanya started to run after Star, but Autumn caught her arm. "She'll be all right. Scherazade is with her. Besides, you couldn't catch her now if you wanted to."

Miss Hernandez and Elaine had spread blankets under an overhanging rock and were opening the cooler. "All the comforts," Miss Hernandez said.

The girls watched the dogs run. They chased each other with bounding leaps. It seemed to Tanya as if they almost flew.

"Forty Acres is a strange name for a ranch," said Elaine.

"I named it Forty Acres because that's what the slaves were promised after the Civil War—forty acres of good land and a mule to work it. The slaves never got either the land or the mule, but here the Salukis can be free. Look at them go!"

The dogs were in close pursuit of a jackrabbit. They had raced almost out of sight toward the hills and were zigzagging back almost as quickly.

"Animals know," said Elaine slowly, as if remembering something. "The land belongs to all life, and life belongs to itself."

"What does that mean?" asked Autumn.

"I'm not sure. It's something my grandmother used to tell me when I was little and caught butterflies. She said that, and then she made me let them go."

Miss Hernandez pointed toward a distant sail of dust cruising toward them across the pale desert floor. "That must be Dr. Storik and the boys," she said.

"Come on," called Autumn, skipping over rocks and cacti down the hill toward the road. Tanya followed slowly. She arrived at the van just as Dr. Storik's red pickup truck pulled to a stop.

Dr. Storik, a short, stout man with wisps of gray in his thick, brown hair, swung down from the cab. At the same time, the back hatch of the camper shell snapped open. Jacob's head and shoulders appeared. He climbed out, followed by a younger boy and two impatient Salukis: a pale cream-colored one Tanya recognized as Terez, and snow-white Deborah with the delicate golden spots. The dogs whimpered and pulled on their leads.

"Let them go. They'll find the others," Dr. Storik called.

"Right," Jacob replied, unsnapping Deborah's leash.

The younger boy released Terez, and the two dogs raced off across the desert toward Scherazade and the rest of the romping Saluki pack. The boys dusted themselves off. Dr. Storik was already on his way up the hill toward Elaine and Miss Hernandez.

The younger boy, a skinny seven- or eight-year-old version of Dr. Storik, folded his arms and stared at Tanya. "Who are you?" he asked.

Jacob gave him a playful punch in the arm. "Remember? I told you about Tanya. This is her."

"Oh!" he said.

Tanya felt herself blushing. What *had* Jacob told him about her?

"I guess I'm better with snakes than people," said Jacob to Tanya. "Sometimes I forget about introductions. This is Bradley, Dr. Storik's son. He helps me out sometimes, don't you?"

Bradley rolled his eyes and scowled. "Help you out? What do you mean by that? Trying to sound like big shot? I'm going to get a soda." He headed toward the shady spot where the adults were laughing and talking.

Jacob blushed a little and kicked the dust with his feet. Tanya watched Deborah and Terez join the rest of the dogs near a group of distant rocks. She could hear their faint barks.

"Aren't you afraid they will get too far away?" she asked.

Jacob shrugged. "We come here every Saturday. We haven't lost one yet. Watch this." He put two fingers in his mouth and gave a shrill whistle.

"Try it, Tanya," Jacob urged.

Tanya placed her fingers at either edge of her mouth and was amazed when a shrill whistle, just like

61

Jacob's, came out.

In a second, all the dogs came running, Deborah in the lead. They surrounded the truck, wagging their tails. Their dripping tongues lolled out of the sides of their wide, smiling mouths. Their noses sampled the breeze and light danced in their eyes.

Tanya gathered a reluctant Star into her arms. The others patted their dogs. Jacob climbed into the back of the pickup and emerged with two big plastic bowls and a jug. He set the bowls on a milk crate in the shade of the truck and sloshed water into them. Autumn had told Tanya earlier that adult Salukis' legs were so long that they couldn't eat or drink off the ground. They had to have their bowls placed on a raised platform of some kind. The dogs gathered around, lapping softly. Jacob set a third dish on the ground for the puppies and filled it with water. Tanya released Star. The pup pushed himself beside Sheik and drank.

Scherazade finished and shook her head, sending water droplets flying, then dashed off across the desert. The rest of the pack took off after her.

Autumn leaned against the truck, staring at the sky. She seemed far away. Jacob sat on the front bumper and threw pebbles, one at a time, down the road. Each of them made a tiny explosion of dirt. Tanya sat cross-legged in the dusty shade, braced herself against a tire, and watched the romping dogs.

She remembered what the article in the dog magazine had said about Salukis. In ancient Arabia the puppies were given to young women to raise for the first two years, then the men took them. From then on, the dogs spent the rest of their lives helping with the hunt. She imagined living in a tent pitched near a giant Arabian sand dune, raising a Saluki puppy for some handsome prince.

Jacob brought her back to reality. He abandoned his post at the front of the truck and stood in front of her, silhouetted against the bright sky. "The lizard died," he said.

"What lizard?" she asked, confused. She struggled to her feet and dusted herself off.

"The one I caught last weekend. Remember? You helped me get the dirt for him." Jacob kicked the truck tire with the toe of his well-worn running shoes. "He died."

"That's too bad," Tanya said.

Jacob shrugged and put his hands in his pockets. "Yeah, it happens sometimes. I keep thinking I'll get used to it, but I never do. I always feel bad, you know?"

Tanya nodded. She knew exactly how he felt.

"I took the other one I caught that morning back to the rock and let him go. I don't like to keep them very long anyway," Jacob continued.

"Why do you catch them at all?" Tanya asked.

Jacob paused, as if the question had never occurred to him. "It's a challenge, I guess. Besides, they're very friendly, and I like to watch them."

"Lizards?" Tanya asked.

"Sure. Did you know that if you keep several of

them together, they will sometimes pile up on top of each other on the side of the aquarium? Each of them has a different way of eating, too."

"What *do* they eat anyway?"

"All kinds of things in the wild, but at home, live crickets or meal worms."

"Yuck!" said Autumn, suddenly snapping out of her trance. "You two are gross, talking about lizards, dead lizards at that. Who wants a soda?"

"Later. Let's go over to the picture cave first," said Jacob.

Autumn glanced at him questioningly. "Already?" she asked.

He nodded.

"Okay," she called, and instantly was off cactus-hopping up the hill toward a rock formation with a few scrubby trees at its base. Jacob followed.

Tanya hesitated. Jacob looked back over his shoulwder. "Coming?" he asked.

"Coming," she said.

chapter

SEVEN

TANYA chose the least prickly route up the hill. She had to watch her step carefully to avoid the long thorns that seemed to cover every tree and bush. There were a lot prickly pears, a type of cactus with wide, fat leaves that grew out of each other. And there was something that Laura had called jumping cholla. Those cacti had prickers that seemed to shoot out of the plant whenever someone got too close.

The ground itself was rough and uneven, strewn with reddish-brown rocks that felt as if they were going to cut through Tanya's boots when she stepped on them. It was slow going, and by the time Tanya was halfway up the hill, Autumn and Jacob were already out of sight.

"Hey, wait for me! Where are you?" she called. The only answer she heard was the irritated chatter of a ground squirrel. He popped out of a hole a few feet away, flicked his curved tail across his back, and disappeared.

She turned to look back down the way she had

come, expecting to see the road and the vans, but the rock outcropping, mesquite bushes, and palo verde trees blocked her view. She heard a sharp cry above her head and looked up. A hawk was circling, shifting his fanned tail.

Tanya felt her heartbeat in her ears. This was real wilderness, she realized, and she was a city kid, all by herself. That was the worst part—being left alone. There was nobody to talk to, nobody to help her. She pushed back a wave of panic and looked up toward the rocks.

She reminded herself that she wasn't really alone. Autumn and Jacob were waiting for her. She just had to keep her head, keep watching her feet, and keep climbing. She would get there. She would tell them off for scaring her; then they would all laugh about it.

The rock formation loomed ahead of her, closer and closer. Finally she was right in front of it. The cliff of weathered, reddish stone stood as high as Laura's porch. The trees she had spotted from the truck sheltered the wide entrance to an arched cave. Still, she didn't see any sign of her friends.

"Autumn? Jacob?" she called, but there wasn't any answer, just the rustle of wind in the bushes.

She stepped inside the cave. It was blackened with smoke from many campfires. Under the soot, Tanya could make out tracings of hands and drawings of strange symbols. Some of them looked like stick figures; others were just shapes, like spirals and circles.

The place was absolutely silent. She couldn't hear the dogs or any voices, only the beating of her own heart. *These are certainly picture rocks,* she thought. *Autumn and Jacob have to be around here somewhere.*

In the distance, Tanya heard a rumble of thunder. She had seen a movie once about flash floods in the desert. They could wash cars away. What if there was going to be a storm and the Roadrunners had to leave? What if they forgot about her?

"Autumn? Jacob?" she called. The dark walls of the cave seemed to soak up her voice, like dry ground soaking up water.

Fears she had pushed to the back of her mind started to come back. What if this was a trick? What if the initiation Autumn had been talking about was to leave her alone here all night? Tanya tried to take a deep breath to calm herself down, but she couldn't seem to draw in any air.

She felt the canteen of water at her side. It would last at least a day, especially if she stayed here in the cave, but what would she do if a coyote came—or a mountain lion?

She looked down past the trees and across the desert. The sky, which had been a perfect blue when they left home, was now speckled with thunderheads, puffy as cotton on the top, and sliced off flat across the base. A gray veil, like a scarf, drifted from the bottoms of some. That veil had to be rain.

A double bolt of lightning branched down from one

of the thunderheads, and the rumble came again. A damp wind rustled the leaves of the trees.

"Jacob?" she called. "Autumn?" The branches and leaves rustled in reply. Another possibility crept into her mind. Maybe there was more than one cave of painted rocks. Maybe they were waiting for her someplace else.

She looked back the way she had come, but she couldn't see the truck. Thinking clearly at last, Tanya realized that since she came up the hill to get here, she could get back by heading down. If the others had left, she could follow the road back to Laura's. She took a deep breath and started down the slope, her heart still pounding in her ears.

She had just passed the trees when she heard it—a low moan. The sound raised the hairs on the back of her neck. She froze in her tracks and looked around. The branches above her creaked and groaned in the wind. Dry leaves whispered and rattled, but the moan had been a different kind of sound, almost human. Suddenly everything around her darkened.

She tried to convince herself it was just a cloud shadow and that she should go on, but she was so frightened, her feet wouldn't respond. She stood there, looking around, desperately trying to come up with an explanation for the weird sound.

The picture caves behind her were dark and empty. Out of the corner of her eye, she saw something move. She scrunched down behind a boulder. It was just a couple of quail.

She stood up, suddenly figuring everything out. The moaning had to be part of the initiation. The two of them were hiding around here somewhere, making ghost sounds to scare her. Well, it wasn't going to work. "Jacob? Is that you? Cut it out," she called. Nobody answered.

The cave looked darker than ever. The handprints and spirals seemed to float in space. Who had drawn them? Could they be a warning that the cave was haunted?

She stumbled down the hill, trying to keep her knees from shaking. The moan came again, louder this time.

She walked faster. The eerie sound continued, blending with the wind. She tripped on a rock and fell to the ground. She stood up carefully. A sharp pain shot through her knee. Her wrist, which she had used to catch herself, ached, but nothing seemed to be broken. She walked more carefully, watching her feet.

As she walked, she heard the shrill sound of another hawk. Of course! That's all she needed to do! Tanya put her fingers in her mouth and tried to whistle for the dogs, but it was hard to get enough breath even to whistle. What came out was more like a whisper. She could hardly hear it herself.

She stopped and closed her eyes. *All I have to do is rest a little and concentrate,* she told herself. The moan came again, right behind her this time. Her heart pounded, but she didn't open her eyes or lose her concentration. She put her fingers at the sides of her mouth and blew as hard as she could. A long, shrill whistle drifted out on the wind.

Sure enough, the Salukis came running, breathless, but eager. To her surprise, they paused by her just long enough for a pat, then continued up to the picture caves. Scherazade and Deborah disappeared behind the rocks. The puppies and Dr. Storik's dog sniffed around the trees.

"Cut it out!" cried a familiar, but irritated voice. "Scherazade, I said cut it out. That tickles." Autumn stumbled out from behind the rocks, her dog dancing triumphantly at her heels.

Deborah, sniffed the air and danced down the hill, then planted herself at the base of one of the trees and barked. "Okay, okay, you found me already," cried another familiar voice. Jacob tumbled out of the branches like an over-ripe apple, laughing so hard he could hardly talk.

Tanya couldn't believe her eyes. She was mad, relieved, and embarrassed all at once. She couldn't stop the tears that were streaming down her face. "You guys!" she sobbed.

Jacob stopped laughing. He pulled a dusty wad of tissues out of his pocket and handed it to her.

Tanya took the tissues and wiped her eyes. Then she wadded them up and threw them back in Jacob's startled face.

"What a creepy trick! I don't believe you did this to me! How could you? I fell down. I could have broken my leg, been bitten by a snake, gotten lost. How could you? Some friends."

She started down the hill again.

"It was great," said Jacob, loudly. "Autumn, you should have seen her face when you did the spook bit. It was perfect."

"Wait, Tanya," Autumn called. "We didn't get to finish."

Tanya stopped. "Finish what?" she demanded.

Lightning flashed and thunder echoed a few seconds later.

"We can't now," said Jacob.

"I guess it's all right. She did whistle for the dogs," said Autumn.

"What in the world are you two talking about?" demanded Tanya.

"The initiation to the Roadrunners," said Autumn. "You're in."

chapter

EIGHT

"WHEN you said I was 'in,' I didn't know that being a full-fledged member of the Road-runners meant doing this!" Tanya complained a couple of Saturdays later. They bounced along in the back seat of Laura's van, surrounded by bags of stuffed animals.

"After braving the wilds and facing ghosts, a party for a few sick kids shouldn't be a problem for you," Autumn said.

"There's one part about that initiation I still don't get," Tanya said. "I mean, it was bad enough that you dragged me out to the middle of no place. But why couldn't you tell me a little something about what was going to happen? You almost scared me to death."

"If we'd told you, it would have spoiled the whole thing. For it to be a real initiation, you had to believe you were all alone out there," Autumn said.

"Well, I hated it, especially the feeling of being abandoned by you guys. You just don't understand. I hate that feeling more than anything," said Tanya.

"You lived, didn't you? You called the dogs all by yourself. I'd say you're braver than you think," Autumn said.

"I'm not brave," Tanya said.

"I didn't say you were brave," Autumn corrected. "I said you're braver than you think—and nicer, too."

"I know what you're up to this time, and it isn't going to work. I'm not nice," said Tanya. "Especially when it comes to spending my whole afternoon with a roomful of little kids with AIDS."

"You said you would help a long time ago, when you first came, remember?" Autumn said.

"You know what really bugs me, Autumn? You always tell me just part of the truth. You said the kids were sick. You didn't tell me they had AIDS," Tanya said. They both leaned and lifted their arms to hold back the stuffed animals as Laura turned a corner.

"What difference does it make?" asked Autumn. "You know that you can't catch AIDS just by hanging around them."

"The difference is that they're dying," whispered Tanya.

"In the first place, they're not all dying and they don't all have AIDS. Some of them aren't even sick. Their mothers are. In the second place, they're just kids. It's a party. Kids love parties. You'll see," Autumn said.

"I don't want to see," said Tanya.

"Stay outside then. See how much I care." Then Autumn whispered, "This is Laura's project, too, though.

She's going to be disappointed."

Tanya knew it was true. She folded her arms and bit her lip to keep from crying. She knew it was mean and selfish of her not to help with the party, but she couldn't help herself. It was the way she felt. She glanced out the window, then made her hands into fists and pounded on her thighs until they hurt.

"I can't. I just can't," she said.

"Fine," Autumn snapped.

The van pulled to a stop and a stuffed patchwork circus seal fell into Tanya's lap. Laura opened the side door. "Here we are," she said, grabbing one of the bags. "If we each take one, that ought to do it."

Tanya and Autumn looked at each other. Autumn grabbed a bag and hopped off the long bench seat onto the sizzling cement. Tanya hesitated, turning the stuffed seal over and over in her hands.

"I couldn't help but overhear you and Autumn talking," whispered Laura. "It's okay, Pony. You don't have to help if you don't feel like it."

Tanya felt something twist inside of her. She hugged Laura, hard. "I don't know why I'm so scared, N.T.," she said.

"A lot of people are," said Laura. "It's hard to think about kids being sick, especially kids you know and like."

"But I don't know them," Tanya insisted.

"You will if you come to the party, won't you?" Laura said.

Tanya watched Laura and Autumn carry their bags

across the parking lot. She took a deep breath, stuffed the seal into the last bag from the back, and followed.

The party was being held in the community hall of the Scottsdale library. It was about twice the size of a classroom, painted a blank white. Watercolors of desert sunsets decorated the walls. The floor was covered by a well-used burgundy carpet.

Two women were already there, setting up folding tables at the front of the room. The taller of the two, a distinguished-looking lady with short, white hair and piercing blue eyes, dashed over to hug Laura.

"Look at this! Just look at this!" she called to her friend, who was shaking out tablecloths. She held up one of the bags, bulging with stuffed toys. "You're a wonder, Laura," she said. "I don't know how you do it."

"Actually I've had a lot of help from the girls," Laura said, turning to Tanya and Autumn.

Tanya felt her face turn red.

"Wait, don't tell me," the woman said. She took Autumn's hand. "I've seen you at the gallery, haven't I? You're Peter's daughter—"

"Yes, I've been to a few of the openings. My name Autumn," Autumn said quietly.

"Autumn, of course," she released Autumn's hand and moved over to Tanya. "Now this is a familiar face—younger, of course, but the resemblance is overwhelming. You must be Elizabeth Marin's girl."

"Tanya," Tanya said.

"Well, well, well. Laura, Autumn, Tanya, we don't have the refreshments set up yet, but if you're thirsty, help yourself. There's plenty of punch. I'm Roberta Winters and this is Gail Woodrich," she gestured toward the other woman, who stopped arranging the refreshment table long enough to nod. "I think you can set up the gift tables over on that side, under the clock."

"Sure," said Autumn heading for the folding tables stacked against the wall. Tanya hesitated.

"It's easier with two," Autumn said.

"Oh, right," said Tanya, hurrying to join her. "I really don't think I can do this," she whispered when they were alone.

"Set up the tables? It's easy. I do it all the time for my mom's parties," Autumn said. Tanya knew Autumn was acting dense on purpose. Tanya gave her an irritated look.

"No, silly, pass out the toys. I don't think I can stand to look at these kids knowing, you know, knowing some of them aren't going to get to grow up," Tanya's own voice surprised her. It sounded like someone else's, shaky and frightened. She felt like running back out to the van, or maybe all the way downtown to catch a bus to the airport.

"You're weird, you know it? You stuffed a lot of these toys yourself. You ought to at least see whether the kids like them." Autumn tipped the long table on its side and pulled out one set of legs.

Tanya snapped out the legs on the other end and they set the table upright. "Stuffing little bears is a lot different from . . .," she hesitated and looked around the room.

Mothers and children were starting to gather at the door. Some were signing in at the guest register and others were wandering toward the refreshment table. Most of them looked like normal, happy children. Some were pale and thin. A few had purple spots on their faces.

Tanya looked back at Autumn, who was standing, hands on hips, waiting for her to finish. "Stuffing little toys is not like this. It's farther away, safer, you know?"

Autumn sighed, then nodded. "Let's just put the animals out on the table, then we can go outside for a while."

"Okay," said Tanya.

Autumn was just putting the last toy, a blue elephant, on the table, when a little girl about three years old came over. Her mother, dressed in jeans and an oversized baseball jersey, was standing back, watching. She looked happy, worried, and tired, all at the same time.

Tanya knew about AIDS. One of her mother's best friends, a director, had died of it. Several actor friends who had brought Tanya toys when she was little were HIV-positive. They had to take special drugs.

The little girl looked really healthy, but Tanya could tell that her mother was sick. The skin of her pale face pulled tight against the bones of her skull. Tanya knew that the new medicines could often keep babies from getting AIDS from their mothers. The little girl was lucky, in a way. But then, in another way, she wasn't so lucky and that made Tanya's heart ache.

She suddenly understood why this party bothered her more than it bothered Autumn. It wasn't just because she had known someone who died of the disease. She also knew how some of the kids here felt—the healthy kids, like this little girl, whose mothers were sick. Tanya's own mother was all she had. If something happened to her, Tanya realized that she would be left alone.

The little girl put a finger in her mouth and planted herself in front of Autumn's end of the table, eyes wide with wonder. She was wearing a pink party dress with a full skirt that flared out a little as she twisted from side to side. Her long, blond hair was pulled back in two neat braids.

Autumn looked at the little girl, then motioned to Tanya. Tanya started to shake her head, but the little girl turned and smiled at her. Tanya stepped around the table and knelt down at the little girl's side. "Hi," Tanya said. The little girl kept her fingers in her mouth, but took one step back. "Do you like stuffed animals?"

The little girl nodded so fast her braids swung around her shoulders.

Tanya glanced up at Autumn, who was smiling, then returned her attention to the little girl. "My name is Tanya. What's yours?" she asked.

"Debbie," the little girl said softly.

"Debbie. That's a great name," said Tanya. "Let's take a look at some of these animals, Debbie."

"Who's that?" Debbie asked, pointing at Autumn.

"That's my friend Autumn. She helped make the animals."

"Ooo," Debbie said, touching a yellow calico lion reverently. She looked up at Autumn. "You made him?" she asked.

Autumn shook her head. "No, Tanya made that one," she said.

"I love him," Debbie said.

"Go ahead," said Tanya gently. "You can have him."

Debbie looked back at her mother, who nodded permission. She picked up the little lion and hugged it close. Then she raced back to her mother, beaming.

"Don't forget to say thank you," her mother whispered loudly enough for the girls to hear.

Debbie, still hugging the lion, buried her face in her mother's skirt.

Tanya watched them make their way over to the refreshment table. The room was filling up and there was a line for the punch. Tanya watched long enough to see Debbie offer the first sip to her lion.

Their stuffed animal table was soon crowded. It was almost an hour before there was a lull in the action. "Hey, Tanya," Autumn said. "Do you still want to go outside for a while?"

Tanya stepped around the front of the display to greet a little boy who was wearing striped overalls. "Are you kidding?" she called back over her shoulder. "I wouldn't miss a minute of this for the world."

chapter

NINE

"WASN'T that a cool party?" Autumn asked Tanya the next week as Jacob shuffled the cards for a game of Crazy Eights. It was cool and dark in Jacob's lizard lab, a welcome relief from the beating sun outside.

"Yeah," Tanya said. "Sorry you couldn't be there, Jacob."

"I'm sorry, too," Jacob said, "but the Zoology Department only offers that lizard class once a year. I didn't want to miss it."

Scherazade, Star, Sheik, and Deborah romped just outside in the old orchard. Tanya could pick out Star's bark, still puppy-shrill when he got excited.

Jacob dealt the eight cards to Tanya and Autumn. Tanya reached for her hand and tried to arrange the cards by suit. For some reason, though, she had trouble concentrating. She couldn't stop thinking about it—the image of herself alone in the desert at the ranch. It was an awful feeling. She had felt as if she was going to die, but she hadn't died. She had called the dogs and she was fine.

Then her mind flashed back to the kids at the party. Some of them were probably going to die, and die alone without their mothers or anyone.

"I got a letter from my mother yesterday," she heard her voice saying as she tried to focus on her cards again. With a little effort, she was able to tell the hearts from the diamonds and the clubs from the spades.

"You got a letter and you didn't tell me?" Autumn sounded genuinely hurt.

"Sorry. I needed some time to think about it."

"Did something happen to your mom?" Autumn asked.

"No, nothing like that. They're going to shoot the movie on location in Hawaii for a week and she wants me to come. She says we'll stay in my favorite hotel there. She only has a few scenes to do, so it will be like a real vacation. Then we'll go home from there."

Autumn picked up her hand and started to arrange it. "Oh," she said.

Jacob ignored the cards in front of him. Then he cleared his throat uncomfortably and stood up to check on one of his snakes.

The old barn was quiet, except for the distant, happy barks of the dogs.

Autumn looked intently at her hand.

"Well?" demanded Tanya at last.

"Well, what?" asked Autumn.

"I just told you my mom is going to rescue me from

this frying pan. Aren't you going to say I shouldn't go?" Tanya asked.

Jacob came over and knelt down in front of her. He put one hand over his heart and looked deep into her eyes.

"Fair Tanya, stay, stay," Jacob said. Tanya could tell he was kidding, but when he stood up, he looked at her again, pleadingly.

"I'll die if you go," Autumn said. She rolled over on her back and stuck her tongue out of the corner of her mouth.

"You guys," said Tanya.

"Oh, come on, Tanya," said Autumn, sitting up and brushing off her shirt. "What do you want? If my mom and dad wanted me to go to Hawaii for a week, I'd go in a second."

"Me, too," said Jacob.

Tanya looked from one of them to the other. She couldn't tell whether they were serious or not. Maybe they already knew what her decision would be. "Would you really go if you had the chance?" she asked.

Autumn paused, then smiled and shook her head. "Not this summer," she said. "I could have gone to Europe, remember? I was exaggerating about Dad working all the time. It probably would have been sort of fun."

"Why would I want to go to Hawaii?" asked Jacob. "They don't have any snakes."

Tanya felt a comfortable warmth in her chest. "Thanks," she said. She looked around the old barn. It seemed as if she had spent afternoons here forever, even though it had only been a little more than a month. Autumn was the best friend she had ever had, and Jacob had become good friend, too—a good friend who just happened to have the most beautiful green eyes on the planet.

Autumn shrugged. "So, when are you going to decide?"

"I already have. I'm staying here," she said. "If I went to Hawaii, I couldn't take Star."

Autumn laughed. Jacob groaned.

Just then there was a scratching sound and a chorus of barks at the barn door.

"Speaking of Star, maybe we'd better give the dogs some attention," said Autumn. "I'll beat you two at cards some other time."

Jacob was already up and out the door. The girls followed him into the bright desert afternoon.

Star and Sheik were romping around together in the dirt, making little dashes, then rolling over and over each other, nipping at flying paws, ears, and tails. They were growing so fast you could almost watch their legs get longer.

"Star!" Tanya called. The pup stopped in mid-growl and perked up his ears. "Here, boy," she said. He rolled around with Sheik one final time, as if to show Tanya he was coming, but that it was his idea, then trotted over.

Sheik shook himself off and ran over to join Scherazade.

"Did you see that?" Tanya asked proudly, giving Star a hug.

"He came the first time I called him," she stroked his shiny black head. "That's a good boy," she said.

"He's smart all right, but watch this," said Autumn. "Sheik?" she called. The golden puppy bounded over to her. "Sit, boy, sit." Sheik stood and looked at her, his mouth open in a wide, panting, dog smile. His bright pink tongue lolled out to one side. "Sit, boy, sit," Autumn repeated. He wagged his long tail.

"That's a great trick," said Jacob. "When are you going to audition that dog for TV?"

"Very funny," said Autumn. "He could do it yesterday."

"Hey, look!" Tanya said, pointing to Star. He was doing a perfect sit. He could have been in a dog show. "What a good baby," Tanya whispered to him.

Autumn shook her head. "Looks like I had my eye on the wrong dog," she said.

"Oh, don't say that," Tanya said, but she hugged Star again, her heart swelling with quiet pride.

chapter
TEN

THE summer was slipping away from Tanya and she hated to let it go. It was already the middle of August and soon she would have to face leaving Phoenix behind. She and Autumn had been spending more and more time at Wind Rock and tonight they had decided to watch the stars come out over the desert. Star and Sheik curled up together and went to sleep. Scherazade sat beside Autumn, her ears perked up, and her nose delicately sampling the breeze.

In the warm silence, Tanya remembered when she had first come up Jackrabbit Hill in Laura's van, how angry she had been, and how lonely. Sitting here next to Autumn and the dogs, Tanya felt as if that trip from the airport had been a million years ago.

Back then, she hadn't wanted to stay one more minute. Now the summer was ending, and she didn't want to leave. Of course, she would take Star with her, but what about Laura, Autumn, and Jacob? Would she ever see them again?

"I have an idea for the Roadrunners' next project,"

Autumn said, breaking into Tanya's thoughts.

"Umm-hmm," said Tanya absently.

"Remember a long time ago when you suggested that we take our dogs to meet the kids? I think it's a great idea. We should take the kids and moms from the AIDS project out to Forty Acres for the afternoon. We could do it the last Saturday before you leave."

An image of the little girl's mother from the party popped into Tanya's mind. She would be even weaker now. Tanya thought of the time her mother had taken her to visit the director friend who had died. He was in a wheelchair and he couldn't feed himself. He was the same age as her mother, but he looked like an old, old man. She didn't want to see that woman again. And she didn't want to see that little girl, especially the day before she had to leave.

"I don't think that's a very good idea anymore," Tanya said.

Autumn had been drawing spirals in the dust with a stick. She rubbed out the drawings with her foot and tossed the stick down the hill. "You're weird. I thought you liked the kids. And this was your idea in the first place."

"Stop calling me weird. You're always calling me that. Maybe you're the one who's weird," Tanya said. Tanya wanted to take the words back the minute she said them. After all, Autumn calling her weird wasn't really what was bothering her. But she could tell from the shocked look on Autumn's face that it was too late.

"You don't have to get all worked up about it. What's

the matter with sharing the dogs? They love everybody—unlike some people I know," she said. She stood up and kicked a stone down the hill, listening to it rattle and bang until it disappeared somewhere out of sight.

"You know a lot about Salukis and the desert, but you don't know everything. You think you know all about AIDS, but you don't. You think you know all about me, but you don't!" Tanya was shouting now and she was surprised at herself.

"How can I know about you when you don't tell me anything?" Autumn demanded. "What do you think you know about AIDS that would keep us from taking the kids to Forty Acres? Do you think the dogs could catch it or something? Because they can't."

Tanya bit her lip to keep from crying. How could Autumn believe she was so ignorant? How could they have spent the whole summer together and still not know each other better?

Tanya was going to tell her about the director, but Autumn had already started back toward the house. "I have to feed the dogs," Autumn said. "You coming?" Tanya jumped up and dusted herself off.

Autumn snapped on her flashlight and Tanya hurried over to where she was waiting. They walked together, the gravel crunching under their running shoes.

"Listen, Autumn," Tanya began.

Autumn froze. She put her arm out and held Tanya back. She played the flashlight's narrow beam down the steep slope behind the house. The light caught a snake slithering toward his hole. Tanya's heart skipped a beat. Scherazade barked, whimpered, and strained at her leash. The two pups looked confused, sniffing the bushes around the dark path.

Autumn kept the circle of light on the snake until it disappeared. When she spoke, her voice was low and serious. "It's a good thing somebody around here cares about other people."

"I can't believe you said that," said Tanya.

"I can't believe you're so selfish," said Autumn.

They walked the rest of the path to the house in silence. Tanya was relieved when they reached the driveway and Laura's automatic floodlight snapped on.

Autumn opened the gate to the small side yard where the dogs stayed. Tanya followed her inside and lifted a big bag of dry food from the storage cabinet, just as she had every evening. She filled all the dogs' bowls and set them on a low platform by the far wall.

The dogs pushed in on either side of Tanya, brushing her with their long, feathery tails. They crunched the dog food nuggets hungrily.

Tanya put the food bag back as Autumn searched the flower bed for the end of the hose so she could fill the water dish. Tanya leaned against the cabinet door and watched Autumn try to turn off the water. That was the hardest job. It was impossible to figure out which way was off. Tanya had been drenched more than once. She found herself hoping Autumn would get it this time. She did.

"I'll get you a towel," Tanya offered, stifling a giggle.

"I don't need anything from you," said Autumn, sputtering.

"Don't you even want to hear *why* I don't want to go to Forty Acres with the kids?" Tanya asked.

"I already know. You're a selfish, spoiled Hollywood brat, and I don't know why I ever wanted to be your friend. I'm glad you're going home in two weeks. I was thinking how much I was going to miss you, but now I'm glad. Do you hear me? I'm glad. I'm only sorry I sold Star to you. He deserves better," Autumn started out whispering, but by the time she finished she was shouting.

The words cut Tanya like a knife. She felt her stomach lurch and her knees began shaking. It hurt— it hurt badly. It felt like the time she almost had Lucky and then lost him. It was as if all of the warmth she had once felt for Autumn turned to a numbing ache.

"Is everything okay down there?" Laura called from the window.

"We'll be up in a minute," Autumn called back.

Tanya swallowed hard and tried to let logic overcome her pain. "Maybe I am selfish, but not the way you think. It's hard for me to talk about some things."

"I don't believe this. I'm standing here in the dark, dripping wet, and you want to have a counseling session." She wiped her hands on an old bedspread hanging on the clothesline.

The dogs were still eating. Autumn held the gate open for Tanya. They both scooted out before the dogs noticed they were leaving.

"Look, can we just talk about this later?" Autumn asked, edging toward the steps.

Now Tanya let her anger bubble over. "No, we can't talk about it later. I used to think Laura called you Speedy because you were a fast runner and a good swimmer. Now I know it's because you jump to conclusions and you don't give other people a chance to explain. You say I'm stuck up and spoiled. I think you're the one who's stuck up."

Autumn rolled her eyes and put her hands on her hips. "I have lots of friends. How many do you have?"

"That isn't fair and you know it," said Tanya, her throat tightening and tears springing to her eyes.

"Excuse me. I'm going to take a real bath," Autumn said. Pushing past Tanya, she ran up the stairs.

chapter

ELEVEN

TANYA lay back on her bed and listened to Autumn's bath running. Moonlight streamed into the bedroom, making the white sheets glow. She had just changed them that morning and they smelled crisp and sweet, but the soft, clean bed didn't make her feel any better. Autumn's words still burned in her heart.

It was Wednesday night and Laura's sewing machine hummed downstairs. Usually, Tanya and Autumn helped Laura on Thursdays. They had settled on the schedule after a few weeks because it seemed to work best. Nobody got in anyone else's way and they all had fun.

Wednesday night was Laura's private time, and Tanya knew it, but she had to talk. She opened her bedroom door and slipped down the stairs. She didn't want Autumn to hear. She wasn't ready to talk to Autumn yet.

The dining room was dark except for a shaft of light that stretched across the hardwood floor from the open door of Laura's workroom. Tanya went to the kitchen first and poured herself a glass of tomato juice. She grabbed a box of crackers from the cupboard and sat down at the counter to think. She wasn't good at having heart-to-heart talks with anyone, especially grown-ups. It was even going to be hard to talk to Laura about this, even though she was one of the most special grown-ups Tanya had ever known.

The hum of the sewing machine stopped. "Tanya?" Laura's voice drifted in from the other room.

"Yes," Tanya said slowly.

"What are you doing all by yourself there in the dark?" Laura asked. "Come on in here and bring me some of those crackers."

Tanya poured another glass of juice, tucked the cracker box under one arm, and headed for the workroom. Laura pushed her chair back from the sewing machine and set up a TV tray. "What a feast," she said.

Tanya put down the juice and crackers and stood awkwardly for a moment, not knowing quite what to do next. Tanya usually felt so comfortable with Laura, but after what had happened with Autumn, she wasn't comfortable with anything.

"Sit, sit," ordered Laura, fishing a handful of crackers from the box. She delicately bit into one, closing her eyes. "Oh, I love these crazy things," she said. She held the box out to Tanya. "Have some."

Tanya shook her head. "I just did. I . . . I really wanted to . . . to talk, N.T.," she said.

Laura put the cracker box down and leaned back in

her chair. "You want to tell me about what happened outside?" she asked.

"Yes, I want to." Tanya twisted a button on her shirt nervously. "But I've got some other things on my mind, too," she finished.

Laura picked another couple of crackers from the box. "Shoot," she said.

Tanya took a deep breath. "I was just wondering, I mean, I've been wondering ever since I got here . . . did you save my mother's life or did she save yours?"

Laura threw back her head and laughed. "That! Oh, Tanya, it wasn't that way at all. It's just a saying, you know?"

"Neither of you was going to die?" Tanya asked.

"Not the way you mean, honey," Laura said.

"What happened?" Tanya demanded.

"It was our last semester at college and I had met the most wonderful man in the world. I was so in love, I was walking around on clouds." Laura's eyes filled with a dreamy distance.

Tanya tried to imagine Laura as a young girl all bleary-eyed over some cute guy, but she couldn't.

Then Laura glanced at Tanya and laughed a little, softly. "The only problem was, I was engaged to another man—a very nice man I didn't want to hurt."

"Were you and my mom friends then?" Tanya asked.

"Oh, yes, best friends," said Laura.

"Like Autumn and me?" Tanya asked.

"Yes, I think very much like that," said Laura. "Your mother was even more beautiful in those days than she is now, which is hard to believe, but true. I introduced her to my fiancé, and that's how she saved my life."

Laura swiveled from side to side in her chair, sipping her tomato juice and keeping her blue eyes on Tanya.

Tanya had the uncomfortable feeling she was supposed to know something she didn't.

Then it hit her.

"Did I know your fiancé?" asked Tanya.

Laura smiled and nodded. "You got it," she said.

"He was my—dad?" Tanya felt dizzy with the information.

Laura nodded again.

"What was he like?" Tanya asked.

"Don't you remember?" Laura asked.

Tanya shook her head.

"Oh, that's right. You were so little. Four, five?"

"I was four," said Tanya.

"He was handsome, just as handsome as your mother was beautiful. He was smart, too. Even in college, he was doing some computer work for the government. The thing I remember most about him, though, was his sense of humor. He could always make us laugh."

"Did he love me?" Tanya asked, her voice very soft.

Laura came over and hugged her. Tanya lost herself in the soft, warm embrace.

"Of course, he loved you, Pony. He always carried you around on his shoulders and told everybody how lucky he was. When you said your first word—I think it was 'nana'—you would have thought someone had found a way to make gold from garbage. He called me up. It was after midnight here, but he called me up just to tell me."

Tanya cried softly then. Her tears came from a place she hadn't ever known about before. And no matter how hard she tried to stop them, she couldn't.

After a long time, Laura got up and walked over to her desk. She pulled out a picture and handed it to Tanya. Tanya had lots of pictures of her father, of course, but this one was different. It was a candid shot, and his expression looked as if he had been telling some sort of inside joke. His smile was warm and easy and his eyes were gentle, but mischievous. There was something warmly familiar about that expression.

Suddenly, Tanya realized what it was. That grin, that sly look—he looked just like her.

Then she remembered how angry she had felt when her mother said he wouldn't be coming home because he had been in an accident. Every time they had to move, she got angry all over again—first at the move itself, and then at him for not being there.

"Autumn thinks I'm terrible. Now you're going to think I'm terrible, too," said Tanya.

"Why, Pony?" asked Laura.

"I hated him," Tanya said.

Laura sighed. "I don't think you're terrible," she said. "It's perfectly normal. You were little. Your daddy left you. How else would you feel?"

"Do you really think so?" asked Tanya slowly.

"Yes, I really do. Sometimes, when we hurt about something, it comes out in all kinds of strange ways. Sometimes it turns to anger."

Tanya nodded. "I think that's what happened with Autumn."

"It sounded as if you two were really upset with each other. You can tell me what it was about, but only if you want to," Laura said.

"I want to," Tanya said, sighing deeply. "You see, Autumn and I had this idea about taking the kids and moms with the AIDS project to Forty Acres to play with the dogs. Only I changed my mind about the whole thing. You see, I didn't want to see one of the mothers there. She's dying, and it's so obvious. I just didn't want to see her." Tanya tried to hold back the second round of tears that she felt welling behind her eyes. "Autumn said I was selfish and spoiled."

"That doesn't sound like Autumn," Laura said. "Did you tell her why you felt like you did?"

"I was going to," said Tanya, "but I didn't get a chance. She just kept getting madder and madder."

Laura gave Tanya another hug, a quick one this time. "Why don't you see if she wants to talk after her bath? Sometimes all friends need is a little time to cool off," she said.

"Thanks, N.T.," said Tanya. She was almost out the door when she thought of something else. "What happened to the other guy? Did you get married?"

"No," said Laura. "But we went out together on and

98

off for a couple of years before he went to New York. He was a playwright. I think he had a couple of productions, but he never made it big—at least not that I've heard of."

"Are you sorry now you didn't marry my dad?" Tanya asked.

"No, baby. It wouldn't have worked. The only thing I feel sorry about is not having a daughter like you. But as long as your mom lets me borrow you sometimes, I'll be happy."

Tanya smiled. She still felt a little weak from all the crying, but Laura's words made her feel warm and strong again. She was ready to face Autumn.

"Good luck with Speedy," Laura called after her.

chapter

TWELVE

TANYA dashed up the stairs to find Autumn. She would start by apologizing for her part in the whole mess. But when she tapped on the door, nobody answered. She pushed it open slowly.

"Autumn?" she called softly. She was surprised to see the lights were off and Autumn's bed was still made.

Clothes lay scattered across the comforter. The sight made Tanya uneasy. Autumn was usually so neat. Every night while her bath was running, she folded everything and put it away. For some reason Autumn had broken her own rule and left her clothes out. *Well,* thought Tanya, *there's a first time for everything. Maybe she was just too mad to pick them up.*

Tanya knocked on the bathroom door. There was no answer. "Autumn?" she called. She turned the door-knob, expecting to find it locked, but it opened easily.

The tub was full, but the bubbles had dissolved. Tanya dipped her hand into the water. It was almost cold. Tanya glanced at the clock by the medicine chest and realized with a shock that it had been over an hour since she had gone downstairs to talk to Laura.

Tanya turned to the towel rack to dry her hands. All of the towels were dry and neatly folded. She checked the clothes hamper—empty. Autumn had run the bubble bath, but she hadn't taken it.

It didn't make any sense. Tanya sat on the hamper for a minute to think. What popped into her mind was her initiation into the Roadrunners. *Of course,* she thought. *This is just another stupid joke. Well, this time I'm not going to get scared.*

Forcing herself to stay calm, she checked her own room, Laura's room, and all the closets. There was no sign of Autumn. When she searched downstairs, Laura came to the door of her workroom. "Looking for something?" she asked.

"Oh, it's Autumn. I can't find her. She's not upstairs, and she's not down here. I don't know where she is."

"Have you checked out by the dogs?" Laura asked.

The dogs, of course, Tanya thought. Both she and Autumn often went out to see the pups at night. "Not yet, thanks," she said, heading for the door.

"Do you want me to come?" asked Laura.

"No, it's okay," said Tanya.

The first thing she heard when she stepped out the front door was Star whimpering. The gate was latched from the outside. Her heart sank. Autumn wasn't there.

When she opened the gate, Star's tail wagged furiously. He strained toward Tanya, but a chain held him back. Something was wrong. She and Autumn never chained the dogs unless they knew a visitor was coming. There was no sign of Autumn or the other two Salukis.

Tanya grabbed Star's leash from its hook by the gate. Over the weeks, Star had grown a lot, but sometimes, especially when he was excited, he acted wild and goofy like the pup that he still was. This was one of those times. He danced around Tanya, wrapping the leash around her legs.

"Stop it, Star!" she cried.

His silky ears drooped and the light went out of his eyes.

"Sit!" she commanded. To her amazement, he obeyed. She untangled herself and knelt down to pet him. "Poor Star," she said. "So happy to see me, then I yell at you. I'm sorry." He licked her hand. "I wish you could tell me where Sheik and Scherazade went, and Autumn, too."

When she said Scherazade's name, Star barked. He wagged his tail and pulled Tanya toward the gate. "Do you know where they are, Star?" Tanya felt a tiny glow of hope. She unfastened the lock and pushed open the gate. Star bolted down the hill so fast, he almost pulled Tanya over.

"Wait! We have to tell Laura," she said.

"It's all right," said a familiar voice above her. Tanya looked up. Laura was wrapped in a robe and she stood on the porch. "You go ahead down to Autumn's house. I'll get dressed and meet you there with the car."

Tanya waved up to her. "Thanks, N.T.," she called

back over her shoulder.

When they reached Autumn's driveway, a motion detector snapped the floodlight on. Tanya followed Star up the steps to the front door. She knocked, but nobody answered. "Autumn?" she called. "Please, give me a chance to explain."

The house was silent.

Laura's car pulled up. "Looks like you need these," she said, dangling a set of keys.

"I don't understand it," said Tanya. "Autumn must be in there. Why don't the dogs bark?"

"There's only one way to find out," said Laura, turning the key in the lock with a sharp click.

Tanya swung the door open. "Autumn?" she called. Star pushed into the room, his delicate nose skimming the carpet. "Look, Star smells them. They must be here," she said.

Laura switched on the living room light. Two fresh sets of footprints crossed the plush rug—running shoes and Saluki paws.

Star led Tanya to the kitchen, where a box of dog biscuits had been torn open roughly. A box of plastic food storage bags sat on the table.

"There's only one dog with her," said Tanya. Her throat was tight and her heart pounded. This wasn't a joke. Something bad had happened. She didn't want to think about it, but she had to.

"You're right. There is only one dog," Laura said. She looked back at the tracks across the carpet. She sighed. "I guess there's no way to tell which one it is."

Suddenly all the pieces fell into place. Tanya knew what had happened. "It's Scherazade," she said.

"How do you know?" asked Laura.

"Star headed this way when I said Scherazade's name. Besides, Sheik has gotten really fast lately. He just takes off. I'll bet he ran off and Autumn went after him."

"She probably thought he would just go home," Laura said.

"Obviously, he didn't," Tanya said.

Star was sniffing at the back door. "I think I should follow Star," said Tanya.

Laura shook her head. "What good are you going to do out there in the dark? That's all I need, two lost kids." She picked up the phone. "I'm calling the police," she said.

Tanya stayed by the door and listened to Laura explain what had happened. She knew Laura was right, but she felt as if she should do something, anything, except stand in Autumn's kitchen and worry.

Laura hung up, then called to Tanya, "Let's go home. They'll bring her home to us in no time, Pony. You'll see."

Tanya nodded and followed her to the car.

chapter
THIRTEEN

IT was a long night. Tanya and Laura sat together in the living room with the TV on. They weren't really watching, but it was comforting to have familiar shows marking out the hours.

Jacob called a little after six in the morning.

"My best friend is lost, and I have to hear it on the radio?" he complained.

"Give me a break," said Tanya. "I'm exhausted."

"Sorry. I just wanted you to know that I called the rest of the Roadrunners. Miss Hernandez will be by to pick you up in half an hour, if that's okay. We'll find Autumn and the dogs. Don't worry," he said.

Tanya felt slightly relieved. Now she and Star would be able to help. Less than an hour later, she wasn't so sure. The Salukis barked and jumped around in the van, but nobody spoke. Even Jacob was quiet. Tanya watched the desert pass the dusty side window. Twin trickles of perspiration made their way down either side of her face.

The van pulled to a stop at Forty Acres. A black-

and-white sheriff's car blocked the road. A man in a dark uniform with a gun, a club, and a two-way radio on his belt met them.

"Sorry, folks," he said. "This area is restricted."

"It's all right," said Miss Hernandez. She explained that this was her land and that the Roadrunners were friends of Autumn's.

"I'll have to check on that, ma'am," he said. He stepped over to the other side of the road and talked on the radio. A helicopter whooshed by overhead.

"Wow," said Jacob. "Are all these guys out looking for Autumn?"

Miss Hernandez nodded. "It's serious, Jacob. She doesn't have any water, and she isn't dressed for the desert. With the equipment, they can find her soon, before—"

"Before what?" asked Tanya.

"They'll find her," said Miss Hernandez, turning away to talk with Dr. Storik and Elaine.

"I'll bet she's up by the picture rocks," Jacob whispered to Tanya. "I'll bet she chased Sheik up there and she's waiting until it cools off to hike home."

"But, Jacob, the search team has probably already looked there," said Tanya.

"With the helicopter flying around, Autumn might think it's military practice. The National Guard comes out here sometimes. They shoot real bullets."

"But what does that have to do with the rescue team not finding her?" Tanya asked.

"Maybe she's scared of them. Besides, these guys

don't know the picture rocks the way Autumn and I do. She could be there and they wouldn't know it." Jacob's whisper was heavy with exaggerated patience.

"You really believe she's up there?" Tanya asked.

Jacob nodded.

"Then what are we waiting for?" Tanya asked. She went back to the van to get Star and Deborah.

The dogs took off across the desert in a blur. Tanya and Jacob followed.

By the time they reached the picture rocks, the helicopter had left. They could hear it whop-whopping its way down the valley. Sometimes they could hear men's voices in the distance calling Autumn's name.

Tanya and Jacob stood for a moment under the cool overhang of the picture cave and looked out toward the desert. Tanya thought about Sheik. Like Star, he was still just a puppy. The desert was huge and dangerous. He could have gone anywhere. Tanya felt numb inside.

Jacob offered her his canteen. She took a swig. Water had never tasted so good. She looked around at the symbols on the walls of the cave. "I wonder which one of these means good luck," she said.

"Probably all of them in different ways." Jacob replied.

"I hope they help us," she said.

"We'll find her. It isn't much farther," Jacob said confidently.

Jacob led Tanya out of the cave and up into the rocks. Her foot slipped on a curved stone. She grabbed a bush to pull herself up. A scorpion crawled out from under it. She screamed.

Jacob took her hand and helped her up the last few feet. He pointed to a shadowy opening behind some bushes on the back side of the rocks. "This is our secret place. I'll bet she's here," he said.

Tanya whistled. Deborah and Star came, but there was no bark from Scherazade or Sheik. "She's keeping the dogs quiet, isn't she?"

"I told you. She might think we're the National Guard. You can't hear things very clearly when you're in there."

"Sure, that's it," said Tanya, trying to keep her hopes up.

Jacob was already making his way down a narrow path to the opening. Tanya followed. When she poked her head inside the dusty cave, her heart sank. Jacob was sitting there, staring straight ahead, holding Deborah.

Star rubbed against Tanya's legs and looked up at her. Tanya patted him. "We'll find them," she said, trying to sound hopeful, but she felt as hollow and dark inside as the cave.

They searched all day and but found nothing. Tanya convinced Jacob to head up to Wind Rock for some inspiration. It was their last hope. They sat side by side on the rocks. Star and Deborah pulled at their leashes, noses twitching. A jackrabbit hopped by and disappeared behind some rocks.

The sun had just set and Autumn's naming wind was starting to blow. Tanya thought about a poem she had memorized in the fifth grade. It was about how you couldn't see the wind, but you knew it was there because it moved things.

A creosote bush twisted stiffly in the breeze. Its rough branches traced a half-circle in the dust. It reminded Tanya of the spiral Autumn had drawn there the night before.

"I have to go home pretty soon," said Jacob.

"I know," said Tanya. "Just help me with this, okay?"

"I'll try, but I really don't know what I'm supposed to do," said Jacob.

"It's easy. Ask yourself where Autumn is, then listen to the wind."

"Sounds dumb," said Jacob.

"Please," begged Tanya.

"All right," he agreed.

Tanya closed her eyes. *Where is Autumn?* she asked herself. She heard the branches of creosote bush whispering, drawing in the sand. In her mind she saw spirals on walls, daughters of daughters of daughters, women grinding corn together, women teaching each other to listen to the wind.

Her eyes popped open. She jumped up. "I know where she is. How stupid! I don't know why I didn't think of it before."

Jacob got to his feet, too. "Don't tell me the wind talked to you. I didn't hear a thing."

"It doesn't talk exactly. It just helps you think," said Tanya. "I'll explain it to you later. Now we have to get up to Hawk Point."

Jacob hit his forehead with his hand. "You're right," he said. "It would have been the first place Sheik would have run to, but it's so close. Why hasn't Autumn come home?"

"That's what we have find out," said Tanya. They stopped by the house to tell Laura where they were going.

Laura was on the phone, long-distance with Autumn's father. "No, no, there isn't really anything you could do," she was saying. Tanya scribbled "Hawk Point" on the telephone pad. Laura waved and nodded. Tanya grabbed her canteen and a flashlight and she and Jacob were off. They ran until they couldn't run any more.

"Let's—walk for a—while," Tanya said, panting.

"We're—almost—there," Jacob replied, gasping. He pointed up the street.

Tanya looked up. He was right. The dark formation loomed against the starry sky. She had an idea. It was slim chance, but worth a try. She put her fingers to her mouth and whistled. Then she called, "Scherazade!"

Two barks echoed from behind the rocks. Star wriggled out of his collar and dashed toward Hawk Point. "Star!" Tanya screamed and raced after him with Jacob and Deborah close behind.

It was dim in the cave on the far side of the rocks, but Tanya didn't have any trouble finding Star. He was nose to nose with Scherazade. Both of their feathery tails were wagging furiously. Just beyond them, propped up against the side of the cave sat Autumn, her face covered with dust-streaked tears.

"Autumn!" Tanya cried. "You're all right!"

Tanya stopped short when she saw the pained look on Autumn's face.

"One of my legs is broken, I think. I can't walk," she said weakly. "And I'm so thirsty."

"I'll go call for help," Jacob said, and he ran back down the road the way they had come.

Tanya handed Autumn the canteen she had brought with her and watched as her friend gulped down the water. Then Tanya put her arm around Autumn's shoulders and gently hugged her. "Sheik got out of the pen, didn't he?" Tanya asked.

Autumn nodded weakly. "I went down to throw some balls for the dogs before I took my bath. I thought it might make me feel better about our fight, you know? Anyway, when I opened the gate, a skunk was going by on the street behind me. Sheik spotted it and took off."

"Where is that dog? I'm going to kill him," said Tanya angrily.

"You don't have to," said Autumn quietly.

"What do you mean? You aren't going to let him get away with that, are you?" Tanya asked, looking around for the golden pup.

"He—he saved my life." Autumn said. She began to sob.

Tanya suddenly felt confused and frightened. "What do you mean?" she asked.

Autumn took a deep breath. "When he started after

113

the skunk, he was running so fast, I couldn't see where he went. I thought he might run home. You know I wear that key on a chain around my neck, so I went straight down to the house and let myself in. He wasn't there. I got some dog biscuits. You know how he loves those. Then I told Scherazade to find him. She led me up here to Hawk Point. Sheik was up on the rocks and he wouldn't come down. It was so late, and I knew you and Laura would be worried, so I started up after him. I thought it would take just a few minutes. Jacob climbs around up there all the time," she paused. "I should have remembered snakes come out at night in the summer."

"Oh, no," said Tanya, feeling her throat tighten.

Autumn nodded her head slowly. "I was going to put my hand in a crevice to pull myself up. A rattlesnake popped out of nowhere. It would have bitten me for sure, but Sheik pounced down on it. He took it in his mouth and shook it and shook it."

Autumn paused. Her face was wet with tears. She choked back a sob. "He was so brave. The next thing I knew, the snake was lying there on the rocks dead, but Sheik was whimpering. It had bitten him in the neck, Tanya."

Autumn took a long, shuddering breath. "I thought I could save him if I got him home in time, so I picked him up and started down the rock, but he was so heavy. I fell. I couldn't walk after that, so I crawled back here into the cave."

"Where's Sheik?" Tanya asked.

Autumn lifted up the edge of her wind-breaker, which was crumpled on the ground beside her. Tanya caught a glimpse of a silky, golden ear.

"He wouldn't have made it, even if I could have taken him home. The venom was too fast."

Tanya was crying now, too. She reached out for Star and he came to her. The three sat huddled in the dark cave, sobbing. Tanya felt his warm breath on her cheek and she ran her hand down his silky back.

She glanced over at the still form under Autumn's jacket and thought about how she would feel if anything happened to Star.

A wave of sadness washed over her, followed by a new, frightening understanding. If it hadn't been for Sheik, Autumn might have died. Tanya thought about their evenings on Wind Rock, their races in the pool, the party for the kids, the trips to Forty Acres, and all the evenings they had sat on each other's beds talking until midnight.

They had shared so much, but Tanya hadn't shared everything. She had held back. In case Autumn changed her mind. In case she was somehow snatched from her, like Lucky had been—like her father had been.

She had almost held back too long.

chapter
FOURTEEN

"SHEIK would have loved this," Autumn said. "He sure would have. Forty Acres was always his favorite place," Tanya said.

They were sitting by the ice chest in the shade of some rocks watching the kids and their parents from the AIDS project pet the Salukis. Jacob was in the middle of it all, introducing the kids to the dogs and explaining all about Salukis. They were too far away to hear exactly what he was saying, but they could tell by the way he stood that he felt very important and very proud.

Autumn had her legs propped up on a beach chair. Everyone had signed her walking cast except Tanya, who wanted to wait until right before she left for home.

"I'm glad you changed your mind about coming," Autumn said.

"I'm glad I finally got a chance to tell you about how I really felt about this," Tanya said. After Autumn came back from the hospital, the two of them should

117

have been exhausted, but they weren't. They stayed up the rest of the night and Tanya had told Autumn everything—about her dad, about her mom's friend, about all the moves, about Lucky. They had both cried, and talked, and then cried again.

"Why didn't you just tell me all that stuff before?" Autumn asked. "I would have understood."

"It's not easy stuff to talk about. I tried to talk about it with friends before, but they changed the subject. A lot of people don't like to talk about depressing things. I guess they think sadness is catching," Tanya said.

"How could you not be sure about me? I was the one who helped Laura organize the party for the AIDS project," Autumn said.

"There's a big difference between stuffing toys for a party and having somebody you love die," Tanya said. "Some people just don't know what to say, so they push you away. I didn't want you to push me away."

Autumn nodded. "I'm afraid you're right. Most people have been really nice since Sheik died, but some have been avoiding me. I understand, but it does hurt my feelings."

Tanya gave Autumn a hug. "You know, you are a real friend, the second real friend I ever had in my life."

"Who was the first?" Autumn asked.

"Laura," said Tanya.

"I heard that," said Laura. She stepped down from the hill behind them, reached into the ice chest, and pulled out a can of iced tea.

"It's okay. I'd tell anybody," said Tanya, smiling. "And then there's Jacob. He's a real friend, too."

"Well, what are we going to do about it? You have all these real friends here and you have to go home on Monday," said Laura.

"I have two weeks off at Christmas, a week in the spring, and all of next summer," said Tanya.

Laura gave her a hug. "You're always welcome at Casa Linda Vista," she said, then she pulled the tab on the can and tea sprayed them both.

Tanya laughed. "A shower. That feels good," she said.

A friend called Laura away and two new customers stepped up to the ice chest. It was the little girl from the party and her mother. This time the little girl was wearing jeans and a T-shirt with a roadrunner on it. Her mother was still pale, but she had gained a little weight, and—best of all—she was smiling.

She picked two cans of soda out of the loose heap of ice. She handed one to the little girl, then she turned to Tanya. "I know you from the party. I'm sorry I don't remember your name, but I want you to know how much that little lion you made has meant to us. Debbie can't get to sleep without it. One day she left it at the babysitter's and we had to drive twenty miles back to get it. I wanted to thank you for being a friend to us. You'd be surprised how many friends I've lost since I've been sick. It means more than you know."

Tanya bit her lip and nodded. She bent down to get a soda so the woman wouldn't see the tears welling in her eyes. When she stood up, Debbie had gone to pet the dogs, but the woman was still there. The tears rolled down Tanya's cheeks. She couldn't hide them anymore.

"It's okay," the woman said. "Really, it's okay. A lot of the time I feel the same way. The new medicine they're giving me is really helping, but it's still hard. Nobody can tell me what's going to happen."

The woman turned to look at the desert behind her. White puffy clouds drifted across a blazing blue sky. Saguaros stood, like men with their hands raised to salute the bright sun. The air was filled with the perfume of mesquite and sage.

Standing beside this woman, Tanya realized how different Forty Acres looked to her now than it had two months before when she was initiated into the Roadrunners. Everything had seemed ugly to her then—strange and frightening. Now the desert felt like home.

"I have a favorite poem," said the woman. "It's called the 'Ninth Elegy' by Ranier Maria Rilke. In it, he talks to the earth as if she were a woman, and he says he doesn't need all her springtimes anymore. He says just one is already more than enough. I feel that way about today."

"So do I," Tanya said softly.

"Me, too," said Autumn, close beside her.

* * * * * *

120

"Hurry up! You'll miss your plane," Laura called from the van. Tanya and Autumn had stayed up all night, but Monday morning had come anyway.

"Just a minute," Tanya called back. She finished her drawing of a spiral on Autumn's walking cast.

"So, will you remember to call, or are you going to be too busy with all of those Hollywood parties?" asked Autumn.

"I'll call. After all, I need to check in on Star. You'll take good care of him, won't you?" she asked, bending down to pet her dog. Scherazade and Star both sat obediently beside Autumn. The training the girls had given them in the last two weeks was starting to show.

"You're right. It was a silly question," said Autumn. "Oh, I'm going to miss you." She threw her arms around Tanya, then pulled back. "Are you sure you want me to keep Star?"

Tanya nodded. "I've never been so sure of anything. Star is a desert dog. He loves the heat and the rocks, and he loves to run. He wouldn't know what to do in the city. And besides, even though he's staying here, I still consider him my dog. I'll be back for Christmas."

"Oh, good. You'll be here for the surprise," Autumn said.

"What surprise?" Tanya asked.

Laura honked the horn of the van. "Tanya," she called.

Tanya put up her hand, "*What* surprise?" she demanded.

"Debbie and her mom are coming to Laura's for

Christmas dinner," Autumn said. "And we're coming, too—all of us. Even my yucky cousin."

"And I'm coming, too," said a familiar voice behind her.

Tanya turned to look into a pair of special eyes. It was Jacob.

"Hmmm," she said, teasingly. "Then maybe I won't come after all." Tanya could see from the hurt look on his face that he didn't get her joke. "You know I didn't mean that. I'm going to miss you."

"I'm going to miss you, too," he said.

Just then, Star whined. The three laughed. "You, too, Star," Tanya said, kneeling and burying her face in his fur one last time. She stroked his ears and he licked her face happily. Then she hugged him again.

Laura gunned the motor. Fighting tears, Tanya turned and ran for the van. She climbed in and waved to Autumn, Jacob, and Star until they disappeared around a curve. The van was very quiet. For some reason, Tanya couldn't think of anything to say. As they headed down the highway to the airport, she was lost in quiet memories.

They pulled into a parking spot at the airport, but Laura didn't get out to get the bags.

"I want you to know something, Pony," she said. "I liked you a lot at the beginning of the summer, mostly because you were Liz's daughter. Now I love you, just because you're you. If anything ever happens—any-thing—you always have a home with me."

"Oh, N.T.," Tanya said. "I love you, too." She hugged

her, even though the gear shift and the steering wheel got in the way.

"We'd better hurry or you'll miss the plane," Laura said.

They climbed out, unloaded the bags, and carried them into the terminal. Laura walked Tanya to the departure gate. "Here's something I want to give you," she said, pressing a flat, square box into her palm.

"This is the final boarding call," called the attendant. Tanya turned and hugged Laura one last time. Then she ran for the plane, the tiny box still in her hand. She settled herself in her seat, and then studied it. It was black velvet with a gold hinge. Slowly, she opened it. Inside was a gold locket with a saguaro cactus engraved on the front. She took the necklace out of the box.

"Fasten your seat belts, please," the flight attendant said.

Tanya pulled the seat belt across her lap. Then she pushed the locket's delicate clasp and it snapped open.

Her eyes filled with warm tears when she saw what was inside.

On one side was a miniature version of Tanya's mother and father's wedding picture from one of Laura's albums. Their faces beamed with happiness. On the other was a tiny picture of Sheik and Star, their ears perked up, their dark eyes gleaming as if they were just waiting for their next adventure.

All About Salukis

The gentle Saluki is a breed of dog with a proud and distinguished past. In fact, the Saluki breed is probably the oldest breed of all domesticated dogs. Its image appears in the carvings made by people in Sumeria (now modern Iraq) some 8,000 years ago. In ancient Egypt, Salukis were considered royal and their mummified remains have been found in tombs next to their royal masters. One of the swiftest of all dogs, Salukis were also used in ancient times for hunting gazelle.

The Saluki breed most likely originated in the Sahara Desert region. In the 1800s, British officers received Salukis as gifts after serving in the area and brought them back home to England. From there, Salukis were brought to the United States where their gentle and loving nature has made them popular pets. Their speed and surefootedness have also made them valuable dogs for hunting and racing.

A Saluki has a look about it that might be described as dignified and noble. Its head is long and narrow and its long ears are covered with silky hair. The dog's long muscular legs are built for running, and Salukis are usually 23 to 24 inches tall. Their ears and tails are also long and are covered with feathery fur. Salukis can be gold, cream, fawn, and black, and they can either be a solid color or a combination of two or three colors.

Like all dogs, Salukis need lots of love and attention from their owners. They are very clean, quiet, easily trained, and very active. To stay healthy, Salukis need lots of exercise, including lots of time and space to run. Because of their desert origins, they are comfortable even in the hottest and driest weather.

If you are interested in learning more about Salukis, contact:

The American Saluki Association
2175 Sterner Road
Green Lane, PA 18054

About the Author

Author Linda Armstrong says, "The idea for *Tanya's Desert Star* was born when my daughter wanted a dog for her elementary school graduation present. She read many books and magazines about different breeds of dogs. She showed me an article about Salukis. The article said Salukis thrive in Phoenix because they love heat and because there is lots of room for them to run. I wrote *Tanya's Desert Star* for my daughter, and for all dog lovers like her who face new challenges year after year. I wish them lots of love and room to run."

A former elementary school teacher, Ms. Armstrong is the author of several magazine stories for children and a book of poetry for adults. *Tanya's Desert Star* is her first novel. She lives in Los Angeles with her husband, her daughter, and the dog her daughter chose, a Shetland sheepdog named Summer.